Poetic Art Presents: STAR GAZING IN GUATEMALA

by Elias Shabazz

This is a work of fiction. Names, characters, businesses, places, events, and incidents are either

the product of the author's imagination or used fictitiously. Any resemblance to actual persons,

living or dead, or actual events is purely coincidental.

Published by Elias Shabazz

2026

ISBN: 979-8-234-05864-5

Cover design by Elias Shabazz

Printed in the United States of America

For permissions, inquiries, or special editions, contact:
mr.eliasshabazz@gmail.com

For the lovers, the dreamers, and the quiet souls

still

waiting for their sky to open.

Table of Contents

"We don't get to pick the sky, only where we stand when we look up."

— Rashad Ali

Cast of Characters

Zeke Ali

Hospital infrastructure & operations consultant. Quietly funny, deeply loyal, more romantic than he wants to admit. Loves Natiruts, notebooks, and making sure buildings don't kill people. Learning to organize his whole life around what's true instead of what's expected.

Reina Delgado

Former nonprofit director turned staff-wellness consultant. Chapina at heart, sharp-tongued, soft-hearted, recovering burnout queen. Loves MC Magic, affirmations, and telling the truth even when it scares her. Guatemala is her oxygen.

Uncle Rashad

Zeke's uncle. Jazz music instructor, unofficial family griot, professional dispenser of hard truths wrapped in metaphors. Loves Miles Davis, his students, and calling out fake friends. Believes in "head, heart, feet, beat" and playing the hand, you have.

Miri Rosario

Reina's best friend. Creative, big-hearted, designer/brand whisperer for nonprofits and small orgs. Loyal to a fault. Survives a brush with Antonio's charm and chooses herself instead.

Tasha Whitfield

Reina's other best friend. HR / People & Culture pro. Reader of patterns, sniffer of nonsense. Dry humor, deep compassion. Climbs into a director role at a healthier organization and keeps everyone honest along the way.

Antonio Sharp

Zeke's longtime "friend." Charming on the surface, quietly jealous underneath. Sabotages with backhanded advice and faux concern. The embodiment of storm energy—useful only in contrast to what real love looks like.

Pup

A Doberman Pinscher with oversized paws, bright eyes, and a heart bigger than he knows what to do with.

Story One – The ONE AND ONLY

"Some people aren't chapters. They're the book you keep pretending you're not writing."

Chapter 1 – Bad Coffee, Worse First Impressions

Zeke Ali met the love of his life in line for bad coffee and mediocre wi-fi.

He was too old to believe in love at first sight, but there was something about the moment that hummed. Not fireworks—more like when a favorite song starts and you recognize it by the first two notes.

The café in Antigua, Guatemala was cramped: white stucco walls, exposed beams, a glass pastry case half-fogged from the humidity. Someone had taped up old, curling concert posters in Spanish. The coffee smelled burnt in a way tourists called "strong", and locals called "overdone".

The line snaked past a fridge, and in its glass door, Zeke caught his own reflection: early forties, average-build, dark-brown skin. His black dreadlocks were pulled back. His bearded face had the softened angles of a man who'd laughed a lot, worried a lot, and lost too much sleep somewhere in his mid-thirties that never quite came back.

In front of him stood a woman who carried herself like a fortress.

She couldn't have been more than five feet tall, maybe less. Black leggings, fresh Adidas, a faded Sonic Youth T-shirt that looked like she'd listened to the band in real time, not bought the shirt at a mall. Her hair was twisted up into a messy knot, short curls escaping around her face. A small gold hoop glinted in her nose.

Her arms were crossed; shoulders slightly angled away from everyone. Her whole body radiated: Don't talk to me, don't try me, don't even breathe too close.

Naturally, he wanted to talk to her.

On his better days, Zeke was friendly in a way that felt natural, not thirsty. It came with the job. Back home in Houston he was a hospital infrastructure & operations consultant—the guy you never saw, who made sure the power stayed on, and the water was clean, and the building didn't quietly kill people. Years of walking into boiler rooms and boardrooms had given him a sense of how to read a space.

Right now, the space around this woman read: Red zone.

He knew that. He pushed anyway.

"Hey," he said. "You in line for the coffee or the wi-fi password?"

She turned just enough to look at him.

Her eyes were deep brown, sharp, and older than her face. They flicked over him in a quick scan: man, alone, chatty, potential nuisance. Verdict: unimpressed.

"Both," she said. "Like everyone else."

Her tone wasn't neutral. It had weight—annoyed, tired, very much not in the mood.

Strike one.

"Yeah, long wait," he tried again. "I heard this place has the strongest coffee in Antigua. Strong enough to make you forget your ex and your student loans, if you time it right."

Debt jokes. Gen X humor. Should've at least earned a smirk.

She blinked once.

"Student loans were paid off years ago," she said coolly. "Exes are old news too."

Then she turned away, conversation dismissed.

Zeke felt the sting more than he wanted to. Not because it was brutal, she hadn't cursed him out—but because it was so casually final. Like he was background noise she'd swatted off.

His ego, that old, jumpy thing, wanted to flare up and say, I was just being nice, what's your problem?

Instead, he made himself breathe. She doesn't owe you anything, the quieter part of him said.

He tried once more, because habits died slow.

"First time in Guatemala?" he asked.

She exhaled through her nose, the slightest audible sigh.

"Does it matter?" she said.

"Not to world peace," he said, keeping his voice soft. "Just making conversation."

"Well," she said, "you don't have to."

That door shut with a satisfying click.

He stepped back half a pace, literally giving her more space in the line.

When the person in front of her finished ordering, she moved to the counter, posture easing by maybe two percent.

"Americano, no azúcar. Y una banana bread, por favor," she said in clean, confident Spanish.

Her voice warmed, just a bit, talking to the barista. It was like watching the sun peek past a cloud and then tuck itself away again.

"Nombre?" the barista asked.

"Reina," she said.

Reina. Queen.

Of course.

Then it was his turn.

"Para usted?" the barista asked.

"Lo mismo," Zeke said. "Y… can you add her banana bread to my order?"

The barista tilted his head toward the woman in black and denim.

"La señorita?" he asked.

"Yeah," Zeke said. "Her."

The barista smirked. "Buena suerte, amigo."

Good luck, friend.

"Story of my life," Zeke muttered.

He paid, grabbed his coffee and her banana bread, and stepped outside.

Reina had already claimed a small metal table, one earbud in, thumb scrolling on her phone. The lines around her mouth had softened now that the social gauntlet was over.

He set the plate down near her hand.

“I think they forgot to charge you for this,” he said evenly. “So, I covered it.”

She pulled one earbud out, looked at the banana bread, then at him.

“I didn’t ask you to do that,” she said.

He nodded. “I know. Consider it… a welcome to Antigua bonus.”

“I’m not new here,” she said. “And I don’t take food from strangers.”

Her eyes weren’t cruel. Just done.

His hands came up in a small surrender.

“You’re right,” he said. “That was presumptuous.”

He picked the plate back up, the banana bread suddenly heavier.

“Enjoy your day, Reina,” he added.

Her gaze sharpened.

“That’s not on my name tag,” she said.

“You told the barista, “He said. “I was behind you. Not stalking. Just listening. I’m Zeke, by the way.”

She said nothing.

He nodded once, to her and to himself.

“Well… have a good trip. Or stay. Or whatever this is for you,” he said, and walked back inside.

He didn't look back.

He wanted to. But for once in his life, he decided not to feed the part of him that turned every woman into a mirror for his worth.

They crossed paths a few more times before Guatemala was done with them. Never long enough to become a story. Just long enough to become a feeling.

Chapter 2 – The Quiet Year

They crossed paths three more times that week.

A ruins tour. She was there, taking photos of broken arches and sky through empty windows. A cooking class. She stood at the back, slicing onions with an efficiency that suggested she'd done more than just follow recipes on Instagram. A bar with a live band playing '90s covers. She sat at a high table with two women—Miri and Tasha, he'd hear later—listening more than talking, posture still guarded.

They never spoke again.

Once, in the bar, their eyes met. There was a flicker of recognition, then her gaze slid past him like he was part of the décor.

On his second-to-last night, he sat on his hostel rooftop, cellphone in hand, staring out at the silhouette of a volcano against a sky dusted with stars.

He called his uncle Rashad.

Rashad answered from his kitchen in Houston, jazz playing low in the background, glasses low on his nose.

"Look at this," Rashad said, squinting at the screen. "My nephew out here on a postcard. You look tired. That mean the trip is good or the bed is bad?"

"Little bit of both," Zeke said, smiling. "I gotta ask you something."

"If it's about politics, hang up," Rashad said. "If it's about love, I'm getting a drink."

"It's not love," Zeke said. "It's... something dumb."

"The dumb stuff is where the good questions hide," Rashad said. "Spit it out."

Zeke told him, in blunt strokes, about the woman in the café. The banana bread drama. The way her refusal had stuck with him like a pebble in his shoe.

"So you like a woman who clearly does not like you," Rashad summarized. "At all."

"Correct," Zeke said.

"And you want to know how to make her like you back."

"Or how to stop thinking about her," Zeke said. "There's nothing there. We barely talked."

Rashad took his glasses off and pinched the bridge of his nose.

"Zeke," he said, "every love story sounds stupid at the beginning. Logic always shows up late."

"You're not helping," Zeke said.

"First thing," Rashad said, "you must respect her no, if she doesn't want you talking to her. That's her right. You don't turn her into some prize you gotta win. No chasing. No stalking. No 'just one more chance.'"

"I wasn't going to—"

"Second thing," Rashad cut in, "if you can't stop thinking about her, that ain't about her. That's about you. Something in her hit a bruise in you. Maybe she didn't bend for your charm, and your ego not used to that. Maybe you saw a kind of strength or wound in her that reminded you of yourself. She's a mirror, not a mission."

Zeke fell quiet.

"What do I do with that, then?" he asked.

"You love in silence," Rashad said.

Zeke frowned. "What does that even mean?"

"It means you let yourself be affected without making them carry it," Rashad said. "You let the feeling push you to grow. You don't turn it into a reason to bother her. If you see her again one day and you're both available and you feel led to talk, fine. You show up different. If she still doesn't want you? You walk. Dignity intact. No villains, no tantrums."

Zeke looked up at the real stars, not the ones filtered through his phone.

"Love in silence," he repeated.

"Quiet love still counts, nephew," Rashad said. "Might be the only kind that grows you."

That night, in his notebook, Zeke wrote:

**Her name is Reina. She didn't like me. That's okay. What's not okay is how much I wanted her to. I'm going to let that discomfort sit with me until I understand it. If I see her again someday, maybe I'll be less thirsty for approval. If I don't, she's just a five-minute character in my growth story. Either way, the work is mine. **

He flew home the next day.

Life resumed.

His weeks fell into patterns: site visits, meetings, arguments with vendors, long evenings with building plans spread across his kitchen table. He was good at what he did. He kept things from breaking, and when they did, he fixed them fast.

On Wednesdays, if work didn't explode, he met Antonio Sharp for a drink.

Antonio had started in the same hospital maintenance department as Zeke back in their twenties. Where Zeke had moved up by digging into the unglamorous details, Antonio had vaulted out into sales and "consulting adjacent" work—never quite clear what he did but always dressed well and somehow always with a new watch.

He had a smooth laugh, a sharper tongue, and a way of making even compliments sound like they came with a receipt.

One Wednesday, a couple weeks after Guatemala, they sat at a bar near the hospital—TVs on mute, low R&B humming.

"So how was your little Central America soul search?" Antonio asked, swirling ice in his glass. "Find God? Find yourself? Find a younger woman?"

"It was a trip, not a midlife crisis," Zeke said.

"Same thing at our age," Antonio grinned. "Come on, there's a story. I can hear it in your voice. You got that 'almost' sound."

Zeke hesitated, then gave him the watered-down PG-13 version of the Reina incident.

Antonio listened, then laughed outright. "So you offered some lady banana bread, she burned you down, and now you're out here journaling about her?"

"Nobody's journaling," Zeke said, heat climbing his neck.

“You are absolutely journaling,” Antonio said. “Look, man, I’m gonna be real with you: women like that? They’re mean for sport. Nothing you do is good enough. They live on the high ground. You dodged a bullet. Guatemala is for fun. You come home and date women who actually say thank you.”

“She wasn’t mean,” Zeke said slowly. “She was... clear. And tired.”

“Same thing,” Antonio shrugged. “You really wanna waste time chasing some 38-year-old with a chip on her shoulder who lives in another country? You’re in Houston, bro. Plenty of women, no passport required. Get your ego fed locally. Leave the vacation characters in the credits.”

It sounded like concern. Like he was trying to protect Zeke from heartbreak.

Underneath, something in it felt... belittling. Like Antonio wanted him to stay in the shallow end.

“Yeah,” Zeke said noncommittally. “Maybe you’re right.”

“I usually am,” Antonio said, clapping him on the shoulder. “Trust me. Women sniff out when you’re too in your feelings. Don’t go soft over a woman who probably doesn’t even remember your name.”

The part that bothered Zeke later was how sure Antonio sounded about that last part.

Because quietly, stubbornly, he knew she would remember.

When he mentioned Antonio to Rashad over dinner one Sunday, his uncle frowned.

“You still hanging out with that boy?” Rashad asked.

“We’ve known each other forever,” Zeke said. “He’s... consistent.”

"So is mold," Rashad said. "Doesn't mean you want it in the house."

"What's your issue with him?" Zeke asked.

"My issue is every time you see him; you come back a half-inch smaller," Rashad said. "That man smiles like he's on your side, but every story he tells ends with you doubting yourself."

"You're reading into it," Zeke said.

"I read people for sport," Rashad said. "Antonio liked you better when you were the mess. Now you're doing the work, and he's handing you reasons to stay messy. That ain't friendship. That's somebody scared you might outgrow them."

The words lodged somewhere deep.

In the year that followed, Zeke still saw Antonio. Old habits were as hard to shake as old friends. But he listened differently. He let Rashad's voice and his notebook be louder than Antonio's laugh.

Reina became a ghost thought. Less frequent, but never fully gone.

Chapter 3 – Reina at 38

At 38, Reina Delgado felt older than that number should have allowed.

On paper, she had done all the "right" things. College. Grad school. A decade at a mental-health nonprofit, climbing from program coordinator to director. Panels, grants, a LinkedIn profile full of buzzwords like "trauma-informed" and "equity-focused."

Off paper, she was tired in a way sleep didn't fix.

Her marriage had ended at 35, not with a bang, but with accumulated silences. No cheating, no scandal. Just two people eroding each other, one small disappointment at a time, until the idea of love felt like a job and neither had the energy to show up for.

After the divorce, she poured everything into work. Then her father got sick. Nothing fatal, but with stubborn, frightening heart failure that turned every flight of stairs and chest discomfort into a potential emergency. She became his unofficial case manager, using all her advocacy skills on behalf of the one person she couldn't bear to lose.

By the time she got on that first flight to Guatemala, she was held together by habit and caffeine.

Her two closest friends, Miri and Tasha, were the only ones who got the unfiltered version.

"You need a break," Miri had said, shoving photos of Antigua across her table one night. "Go somewhere pretty that isn't an office with bad furniture."

"Change your scenery or you're going to start biting your clients," Tasha added.

Reina went.

In Antigua, she'd been numb. Every man who tried to chat her up felt like another emotional invoice she couldn't pay. The guy in the café—Zeke—had just been one more demand on batteries that were blinking red.

She hadn't remembered his exact words that day. She remembered the feeling: intrusion, expectation, a quiet assumption that she owed him something in return for his niceness.

So, she'd shut it down. Hard.

Months later, back in Texas, sitting at Miri's kitchen table over takeout, she told them about "Banana Bread Guy."

"He tried to buy my snack like I was supposed to be grateful," she said, stabbing her fork into salad. "Then he said my name like he'd earned it just because he overheard me at the counter."

"And?" Miri asked.

"And I don't take food from strangers," Reina said. "Or validation."

"You also said he didn't argue when you said no," Tasha reminded her. "He didn't 'nice guy' you."

"That's the bare minimum," Reina said.

"It is," Tasha agreed. "And it still messed with you, because you're used to either being chased or ignored. Quiet respect is confusing when you're running on old scripts."

Reina gave her a look. "Did you memorize my therapy notes?"

"I didn't need to," Tasha said. ". I've watched your life."

That night, in bed, Reina thought of Zeke's face—not the flirting attempt, but the moment after, when he'd said, "Enjoy your day, Reina," and walked away without trying to make her feel guilty.

It had unsettled her. Not because he'd done anything wrong.

Because it had shown her how many men before him had.

She kept that thought to herself.

When she finally quit the nonprofit a few months later, burned out to the bone, Guatemala came back to mind—not the man, but the sky, the streets, the strange, clean ache of the place.

She went back. Not for him. For herself.

Found a small apartment she could afford between gigs. Started doing consulting for smaller organizations—staff wellness, boundary-setting, practicing the things she used to preach.

It was less money, less prestige, more uncertainty.

It was also the first time, as an adult, that her nervous system felt like anything approaching quiet.

She was still lonely, but it was at least an honest kind of lonely.

A year passed the way hard years do—quietly on the outside, heavily underneath. By the time Guatemala called him back, Zeke was not the same man who had once stood in a café line holding banana bread and a bruised ego.

Chapter 4 – Second Chances in Disguise

Almost a year to the week after his first trip, Zeke flew back to Guatemala.

This time it wasn't an escape. It was a work assignment: the hospital network had greenlit a sustainability and infrastructure visit. A small team would visit hospitals in Guatemala and surrounding countries to learn how they kept systems going with constrained resources.

It was exactly Zeke's kind of project.

On the plane, he watched the volcanoes rise through the clouds and wondered, briefly, if the city would feel different now that he wasn't walking through it with his own burnout smoking behind him.

His phone buzzed before takeoff.

Rashad:

You up there touching the clouds yet?

Zeke:

Just about.

Rashad:

Remember: second chances come dressed up as regular days. Pay attention.

Zeke smirked, pocketed the phone, and turned it off as they started to descend.

In Antigua, their first afternoon was free.

He walked.

Past markets strung with woven textiles. Past kids chasing a deflated soccer ball. Past tourists with cameras and locals with groceries and the same old dogs sleeping in new spots.

He turned a corner and saw the café.

Same chipped blue door. Same faded, hand-painted letters promising the best coffee in town. Even the crooked sign above the door seemed to be hanging at the same resigned angle.

"Of course," he muttered. "Why not."

He almost kept walking.

Then he thought about his notebook. About Rashad's "love in silence." About the man he'd been last year versus the man he'd been trying to become.

He went in.

The inside felt a little smaller now. Or maybe he just took up more space in his own skin.

He ordered in better Spanish this time, Americano con un poco de leche, and didn't apologize for his accent.

He took a table near the back and opened his notebook, sketching questions for the hospital visits. Boreholes. Gravity tanks. Solar arrays. Backup generators cobbled from salvaged parts.

He was halfway through a sentence when a familiar voice hit his ears.

"Americano, no azúcar. Y pan de plátano, por favor."

He went still.

He looked up.

She stood at the counter, profile as familiar as a song you haven't heard in a while but still knows all the words too.

Same Sonic Youth T-shirt, though this time layered under an open denim shirt. Same small gold hoop in her nose. Her hair was shorter now, brushing her jaw; it framed her face in a way that made her look both younger and more defined.

She stepped aside with her plate and cup, scanning the room as always. Checking exits. Testing the air.

Her eyes landed on him.

Recognition flared. Surprise first. Then the beginnings of that old defensive lift in her shoulders.

He had a second to choose.

Antonio's voice floated up first, uninvited:

*"Leave the vacation characters in the credits. Don't be that guy chasing some 38-year-old in another country." *

He let that thought pass like static.

Rashad's voice followed, steadier:

"Be yourself—but the version that's been doing the work."

He closed his notebook.

He stood.

He walked toward her, heart surprisingly calm.

"Reina," he said, stopping far enough away that she wouldn't feel crowded.

Her eyes narrowed for a heartbeat, then widened.

"Zeke, right?" she said.

That she remembered his name hit him like a small, quiet meteor.

"You remember me," he said.

"I remember details," she said. "Comes with the job."

"What is the job now?" he asked.

She hesitated. "Used to be nonprofit director. Now it's… consultant, occasional troublemaker, full-time burnout recovery project."

"That sounds… accurate," he said.

The barista plunked both their drinks on the counter at the same time.

They stepped in, dodged each other, then both half-laughed at the awkward mirror of it.

"You first," he said, stepping back.

She picked up her coffee and the banana bread, then looked at him over the rim of the cup.

"You're back," she said.

"For work," he said. "Hospital infrastructure consulting. And you?"

"I… live here now," she said. "Mostly. Guatemala and Texas. It's complicated."

"I've got time, if you want to explain," he said. Then he added quickly, "If you don't, that's okay too."

She studied him like he was a painting she wasn't sure she liked yet.

"You're different," she said finally.

"Better, I hope," he said.

"Less... auditioning," she said.

He smiled at that. "Retired from auditions. Union rules. Now I just play myself."

A tiny flicker of amusement crossed her face.

"Let's sit," she said. "You owe me the short version of why you're still thinking about a woman who once verbally karate-chopped your banana bread."

He laughed. "Fair."

They found a small table by the window and sat.

A moment passed where neither spoke.

"I owe you something," he said.

Her shoulders tensed. "We barely spoke."

"Exactly," he said. "I still turned you into a character in my head. The cold woman in the café. The villain in a five-minute rom-com I wrote by myself. That wasn't fair."

Her gaze sharpened.

"You thought I was a villain because I didn't want your pastry?" she asked.

"I thought I was entitled to a conversation," he said. "You reminded me I wasn't. My ego didn't like it. But my better self needed it."

She sat back.

“Men don’t usually come back after a year to admit THAT,” she said.

“Men don’t usually have an Uncle Rashad,” he said. “He told me to ‘love in silence.’”

She tilted her head. “That sounds like a Prince song.”

“It should be,” he said. “He meant I could let your impact be about my growth—not your responsibility. You didn’t ask to be in my little emotional independent film.”

Her jaw worked like she was holding something back. Then she sighed.

“I was in a bad place last year,” she said. “You didn’t deserve the full blast of that.”

“You were clear,” he said. “Not cruel. Just... self-protective. Given what I know now, it tracks.”

“What do you know now?” she asked.

“That you didn’t come to Guatemala to audition strangers for the role of Guy Who Buys You Banana Bread,” he said. “And that my need to be liked is not your problem to fix.”

The corner of her mouth curved up, almost involuntarily.

“Okay,” she said. “That’s... actually decent self-awareness.”

He put a hand to his chest. “Careful. Compliments like that go straight to my head.”

She rolled her eyes, but it didn’t land as harshly this time.

Chapter 5 – Old Stories, New Mirrors

They traded life summaries.

She told him about the decade in nonprofits, the marriage that dissolved so quietly it barely made a sound, her father's heart failure, the way she'd turned her entire nervous system into a 24/7 emergency response unit until it finally gave out.

"I came back here because it was the only place in my brain that didn't feel like a triage room," she said.

"And now?" he asked.

"Now I help small organizations not become the monster that almost ate me alive," she said. "Staff wellness. Boundaries. Saying 'no' before burnout becomes policy. I make less money and sleep more. Both still feel weird."

He nodded. "Sounds like healing."

"Sounds like drifting," she countered. "But at least the drift is mine."

He told her about starting as the kid changing filters and fixing leaky pipes in a hospital basement, how he'd worked his way up until administrators listened when he said, if we don't replace this, something bad will happen. How he liked being the invisible backbone instead of the face on the brochure.

He talked about almost getting married once, in his thirties, to a woman who'd been brilliant and wounded and chaos in beautiful packaging.

"I realized I was more in love with the idea of saving her than of being her partner," he said. "When she started to get better, I didn't know who I was if I wasn't fixing something."

"Co-dependency chic," Reina said softly. "I know that line."

They both smiled at the shared language of people who'd been to therapy and taken notes.

Time slipped. People came and left around them. Coffee cups emptied, crumbs of banana bread disappeared, and still the words kept coming.

At some point, two familiar voices cut across the café noise.

"Reina!" Miri called, then pulled up short when she saw Zeke.

Behind her, Tasha raised an eyebrow, eyes flicking between them.

"Oh," Miri said slowly. "Is this...?"

Reina pinched the bridge of her nose. "Yes. This is Banana Bread Guy."

Zeke lifted a hand. "Guilty."

Tasha grinned. "We've heard a... very anti-banana bread version of your story."

"I deserve that," he said. "I led with pastry, not consent."

Miri laughed. "I like him already."

"We're just talking," Reina said, unnecessarily defensive.

“Talking is allowed,” Tasha said, sliding into a spare chair. “As long as he knows we will absolutely run a background check with Uncle Rashad.”

“You’ve already got an in with my uncle,” Zeke said. “He doesn’t like my friend Antonio. You’re automatically ahead.”

“Antonio?” Reina asked.

“Old work friend,” he said. “My uncle calls him ‘the man with the butter knife smile.’”

“That’s ominous,” Miri said.

“Accurate,” Zeke said.

Reina watched him for a moment as he bantered with her friends. He wasn’t pushing. Wasn’t turning on some exaggerated charm to win them over. He listened when they spoke, laughed when it was warranted, didn’t take over.

He wasn’t who he’d been in line a year ago.

Something in her unknotted a little.

Chapter 6 – Hospitals & A Shooting Star

Over the next week, they wove in and out of each other's days.

Reina joined Zeke and his colleagues on a visit to a regional hospital where she'd once done a staff workshop. She moved through the corridors like she belonged there—greeting nurses, checking in with admin, explaining to his team how cultural expectations shaped what staff would complain about versus what they'd silently endure.

Zeke watched her with a quiet respect that had no trace of savior in it.

Later, she watched him deep in a mechanical room, headlamp on, peering into an ancient panel while the local maintenance tech pointed things out.

"You light up when you talk about backup systems," she said that night over cheap tacos.

"Somebody has to," he said. "If the power stays on, NICU babies live. If the water stays clean, there are fewer infections. I don't touch patients, but if I do my job, the room doesn't hurt them."

"That might be the most romantic description of a generator I've ever heard," she said.

"Infrastructure romance," he replied. "Highly underrated."

They walked under Antigua's sky after dinner, stars scattered thickly as if someone had spilled salt across black velvet.

On his hotel's rooftop later, they sat side by side on a low wall, shoulders almost touching, both looking up.

"Do you ever think," she said, "that we're just extras in someone else's movie? Background walkers in some main character's big scene?"

"I used to," he said. "Now I think we're all main characters who wander into and out of each other's stories. Even the background people change your plot more than you know."

She hummed.

A streak of light cut across the darkness.

He pointed. "Shooting star."

"Or space trash burning up," she said. Then, softer: "But yeah. Let's be poetic and call it a star."

He glanced at her profile. The way her jaw relaxed in the dark, how different it looked from the clenched version he'd seen a year before.

"Make a wish," he said.

"I don't wish on things that can't answer back," she replied. "Stars, men, institutions. Learned my lesson."

He smiled. "Fair."

Still, she closed her eyes for a second. When she opened them again, they were a little brighter.

In his chest, something quiet and steady grew. It wasn't the frantic high of infatuation. It felt like watching a light come back on in a room that had been dark too long.

Chapter 7 – Antonio, Again

Back in Houston, after that week, their rhythms shifted.

They texted. They called. Sometimes they just left each other voice notes—little slices of life: a dog barking on her street, a mechanical room hum behind him, a random '90s song playing in a grocery store that made them both feel 17 and 47 at the same time.

Zeke mentioned it to Antonio one Wednesday at the bar.

"So, you actually went back and found this woman?" Antonio said, eyebrows raised. "You are really committed to this side character."

"I didn't find her," Zeke said. "I just... saw her. Same café. We talked. It wasn't some dramatic thing. Just... honest. It felt good."

Antonio took a sip of his drink, lips pressed.

"And now what?" he asked. "You gonna do long-distance with a woman who lives in another country and once iced you over baked goods?"

Zeke's jaw tightened. "It's not like that anymore."

"Look, man," Antonio said, voice softening into that fake-concern tone Rashad hated, "I'm happy you're... trying something. But be smart. You work a lot. You don't have time for telenovela drama. Women like that? High expectations. Always testing you. You really want to sign up for that when you could just meet someone here who actually shows up in person more than twice a year?"

Zeke stirred his drink.

"You sound like you're looking out for me," he said, "but it keeps landing like you think I should expect less."

"I think you should avoid heartbreak," Antonio said. "Some of us care about you more than your uncle's starry-eyed nonsense."

Later, walking into Rashad's kitchen, Zeke replayed that "more than your uncle" line and felt his shoulders bunch.

Rashad didn't sugarcoat it.

"Antonio likes you better miserable," Rashad said when Zeke told him. "Some folks feel taller standing next to someone hunched over. You start standing up straight, they get itchy."

"You think he's... jealous?" Zeke asked, like he was trying on the word.

"I know he is," Rashad said. "Because he's still playing at life, and you're finally living it. Don't let a man who's scared of depth coach you on how to swim."

When Reina came to Houston for the first time, it felt surreal.

He picked her up from the airport, both of them doing that stiff little dance of people who'd been intimate in conversation but not yet in shared space over days.They spent the weekend in what Reina would later call the "PG-13 star gazing phase"—lots of talking, hand-holding, some kissing that made both of them feel like teenagers and elders at once.

One night, they met some of Zeke's people at a bar. Antonio, of course, showed up.

"Zeeeeeke Ali," Antonio sang out, hugging him. "And this must be the infamous Guatemalan glitch."

Reina's brows lifted. "I'm not from Guatemala," she said.

“Technicalities,” Antonio said. “You’re the banana bread ghost.”

“Wow,” Zeke muttered. “Way to make that weirder.”

“I’m kidding,” Antonio said smoothly. “I’m happy for you, man. You finally found someone who can handle all your… intensity.”

Reina clocked the pause before intensity.

Smiled a cool, polite smile. Filed it away.

The next morning, over brunch with Miri and Tasha, she didn’t hold back.

“Antonio?” she said, stirring her coffee. “He smiles with his mouth, not his eyes.”

Tasha snorted. “We hate that.”

“He kept making jokes that sounded like compliments but shrunk Zeke every time,” Reina said. “Like he needed everyone to remember who Zeke used to be.”

“Some people are addicted to your old version,” Miri said. “Your growth makes them dizzy.”

“Uncle Rashad already said he doesn’t like him,” Reina added. “Which tells me everything I need to know.”

If love was learning how to move toward what was good, temptation was often much quieter. It smiled easily. It listened closely. It arrived looking almost familiar.

Chapter 8 – Miri & Antonio

Later that same weekend in Houston, Reina and Zeke hosted a small get-together at Zeke's place. Nothing fancy—vinyl records, takeout, half-burned candles on the coffee table.

Antonio showed up late, as if on purpose.

"Sorry, sorry," he said, stepping in with two bottles of wine and an overdone bow. "Had to fight Houston traffic and my own bad decisions."

"Traffic I believe," Tasha said. "The other part is redundant."

They laughed. It was easy to laugh around Antonio at first. That was part of the problem.

At some point, the group splintered. Rashad commandeered the turntable, talking jazz theory with Zeke in the kitchen. Reina and Tasha sat on the balcony, talking about her dad's latest cardiology appointment.

That left Miri in the living room with Antonio and a mess of empty plates.

"I'll help," she said, stacking them.

"Look at you," Antonio said, grabbing a few. "Doing unpaid emotional labor and unpaid dish duty. You must be quality people."

"Or just tired of looking at chicken bones," she said.

They carried plates to the sink. The kitchen was crowded, so they detoured to the dining table instead, setting everything down.

“You do design, right?” he asked, leaning against a chair. “Reina mentioned something about you making boring nonprofits look less boring.”

Miri tilted her head. He remembered that? “Yeah. Branding, digital stuff. Websites. Social. I try to help them not look like they were built in 2003.”

“I’d hire you,” he said. “Half the companies I work with still think a logo is just putting their name in Times New Roman.”

“What do you actually do?” she asked. “Zeke keeps saying ‘consulting,’ but that can mean anything from saving the world to selling vapor.”

He chuckled. “I’m… between gigs at the moment.”

“In between what and what, though?” she pressed, genuinely curious.

“You’re nosy,” he said, but his eyes were amused. “I like that. Okay—truth: I used to do sales for a facilities firm. Now I help connect people, projects, and money. Middleman with better suits.”

“Professional middle child,” she said.

“Exactly.” He smiled, and this time it reached his eyes a little. “It pays the bills, most days. You ever feel weird that your art is tied to other people’s budgets?”

“All the time,” Miri said. “I make things pretty for organizations that sometimes barely know what they’re doing. But when it lands—when a client says, ‘People actually understood us because of this’—that part feels… good.”

His gaze softened. “See? Quality people.”

She felt her cheeks warm and hated that.

From the balcony, she could see Reina through the glass door, mid-conversation with Tasha. She thought of how they'd dragged Antonio earlier, how quickly they'd pegged him as dangerous to Zeke's peace.

And here she was, feeling a small pull toward him because he'd listened to her talk about fonts.

"You and Zeke go way back," she said, redirecting.

"Since we were kids in coveralls," he said. "I was the one saying we'd be running the building one day. He was the one actually making sure the lights stayed on."

"You proud of him?" she asked.

"Sure," Antonio said, with a little shrug. "He found his lane. He's… stable. Reliable."

The way he said it, reliability sounded like a participation trophy.

"You don't sound proud," Miri said.

He glanced at her, caught.

"I'm happy for him," he said. "I just… don't want to see him get played. Reina seems cool, but long-distance? Woman with half her life in another country? That's a lot of risk for a guy who still writes in a notebook like it's 1999."

Miri bristled, just a bit. "Reina's not playing him."

"You know that?" he asked lightly.

"I know her," Miri said. "She doesn't do half-in."

He held her gaze for a moment, then smiled.

"See? Loyal," he said. "Told you I respect that."

He stepped a little closer, not enough to be inappropriate, just enough that she could smell his cologne—clean, expensive, a little too intentional.

"You ever get tired of being the loyal one?" he asked quietly. "Always the friend, never the main event?"

The words landed too close to home.

She laughed it off. "Wow. You are psychoanalyzing me now?"

"Occupational hazard," he said. "People person. I read the room."

Miri swallowed, hating that a tiny part of her wanted to keep talking to him alone. Hating that he'd said out loud the thing she only whispered to herself on bad nights: When is it my turn?

From the kitchen, Rashad's voice cut through, warm and sharp.

"Antonio!" he called. "Come argue with me about whether Coltrane peaked in '61 or '65!"

Antonio winked at Miri. "Saved by the jazz man."

He moved away, his attention shifting in that easy way that made everyone feel briefly spotlighted and then abandoned.

Miri stood there a second longer, heart beating faster than a simple dish run should warrant.

Later, when she lay in the guest room Reina had set up for her, staring at the ceiling, she thought about his question.

Always the friend, never the main event?

She thought about how disgusted she'd been with herself, just a little, for even feeling drawn to someone she knew in her bones was not good for Zeke.

In the morning, when Tasha asked, "So, what did you think of Antonio really?" Miri just said, "He's exactly the kind of man I tell my clients to avoid."

She didn't add: And exactly the kind of man a very small, very tired part of me still finds magnetic.

She filed that away for later.

The universe, as usual, was paying attention.

Chapter 9 – Star Gazing

On Zeke's second-to-last night of that first true "we're actually doing this" season, back in Antigua months later, they sat in the town square again.

Vendors packed up. A guitarist played something soft and familiar from the '90s near the fountain. Lanterns flickered to life around them, painting everything in warm, forgiving light.

"I need to say something before I talk myself out of it," Zeke said.

"You're giving Very Special Episode energy," Reina said. "I should be worried, right?"

"A little," he said, smiling. "But hopefully in a good way."

She folded her arms. "Okay. Hit me."

"I like you," he said.

She rolled her eyes. "We've established that."

"Not as an idea," he continued. "Not as the woman who rejected my pastry. I like you. Reina Delgado. Thirty-eight. Burned out and unburning. The woman who left a job, a marriage, and a whole expectation structure rather than die slowly inside it. The woman who will absolutely call me on my BS even when it would be easier to smile and nod."

Her throat bobbed.

"I don't want to pretend this is casual and then carry that lie home with me," he said. "At our age, playing it cool just leads to lukewarm lives."

"You rehearsed that," she said quietly.

"I did," he admitted. "Because I'm scared. And because I've decided I'd rather risk sounding corny than stay silent and regret it later."

She stared at him, brown eyes glistening.

"What do you want from me, exactly?" she asked.

"I want to keep trying," he said. "For real. Long distance. Slow. Honest. Houston, Guatemala, star gazing via FaceTime and under actual skies. Maybe one day, the other kind of star gazing too."

Her lips parted. "The other kind?"

He swallowed but pushed through.

"Look," he said, "sex matters. Not just the physical, but what it means. I don't want another half-present hookup. If we get there, I want it to feel like it is—two grown people choosing to be fully in their bodies and their hearts with each other. Making love, not just... trading trauma."

She blinked, then laughed once, startled.

"No one says 'making love' anymore without irony," she said.

"I'm bringing it back," he said. "Retro. Like everything else we grew up with."

She shook her head, but she was smiling through the nerves now.

"I don't know how to do that," she said. "The healthy version. I know how to have sex to prove I'm wanted. I know how to withhold it to prove I have control. I don't know how to… star gaze the way you're talking about."

"Me neither," he said. "But I'm willing to learn. Slowly. With you."

Silence stretched. Thick, not empty.

"I'm scared of fighting," she admitted. "My marriage was one long, low-level war. I don't know how to have conflict that doesn't mean the end is coming."

"And I'm scared of being needed in ways I can't carry," he said. "I've over-functioned, tried to be everything, and then resented people for letting me. I don't want to make you, my project. I want to be your partner."

Her eyes shone.

"Who taught you to talk like this?" she whispered.

"Rashad. Therapy. And a woman in a café who refused my banana bread," he said. "In that order."

She laughed, wiping at one eye.

"This is insane," she said again.

"Yeah," he said. "So is getting on a plane. So is letting someone see you first thing in the morning without caffeine. Most good things are a little insane."

She drew in a long breath and let it go.

"Okay," she said. "We try. We text. We call. You come back. Maybe I will come to Houston again. We haven't promised forever yet. We promise effort. We promise no ghosting, no villain monologues."

He nodded, feeling something settle into place inside him like a click.

"Deal," he said softly.

She slid her hand into his.

It was small, cool, and shaking just enough to prove this mattered.

"Don't make me regret this, Zeke Ali," she said.

"I've done enough regretting for one lifetime," he replied. "I'd rather spend the rest of it finding out what happens when we actually show up."

Above them, the Guatemalan sky glowed, full of stars neither of them needed to wish on anymore.

They'd been wishing for years—in the wrong places, on the wrong people, on versions of themselves that didn't exist yet.

Now, under that sky, they weren't making a wish.

They were making a choice.

To fight, gently but insistently, for this strange, late-found thing between them.

To fight against old scripts, against saboteurs in friendly clothing, against the urge to run at the first sign of fear.

To fight for the one and only chance they had at being fully themselves—with each other.

Years later, when they'd talk about the night their lives really turned, they wouldn't say we fell in love. They'd say:

"That was the first night we really started star gazing."

And both would know they meant the sky.

And the other kind.

And the sacred space in between.

Story Two – REINA DEL CIELO

"Heaven isn't up there. It's the place where you can be fully human and still stay."

— Rashad Ali

Previously, in "THE ONE AND ONLY" ...

Zeke Ali met Reina Delgado in a cramped café in Antigua, Guatemala, where his attempt at banana-bread charm crashed into her burnout and razor-sharp boundaries. He went home, got called out by his jazz-instructor uncle, and spent a year quietly leveling up. She went back to a life of responsibility, loss, and emotional airplane mode.

A year later, the universe queued up a remix: same café, same city, different versions of both of them. This time, he apologized without demanding forgiveness, she listened without pretending not to care, and they slowly let each other in.

By the time they left Guatemala, they had not just chemistry but a choice: to try for real, long-distance and painfully honest. No paper, no rings, just a daily, grown-folks yes.

Now they must find out what that yes costs—and what it's worth.

Chapter 1 – Pure Being

I Am a Pure Being of Light and Love, guided by Source Creator at ALL times....

Reina repeated it silently, syncing each word with her breath. Inhale on Pure Being of Light, exhale on guided by Source Creator at ALL times.

The cheap meditation app voice had told her to "anchor the affirmation in your heart center."

Her heart center, at the moment, felt more like a crowded waiting room: old fears flipping through dog-eared magazines, new anxieties pacing back and forth.

Again, she told herself. I Am a Pure Being of Light and Love, guided by Source Creator at ALL times....

The rooftop air in Antigua was cool against her bare arms. Below them the city hummed: a scooter whining down cobblestones, someone laughing too loud in Spanish, distant reggaeton from a bar three streets over. Somewhere, a trumpet played a clear, wandering line—some kid practicing in his room or a band warming up.

Beside her, Zeke lay flat on his back on a thin blanket, hands behind his head, eyes on the sky.

"You praying or plotting?" he asked, not turning.

"Both," she said, pulling one earbud out. "Affirmations. Therapist homework."

"Fancy prayers," he said. "Therapist-approved."

She turned her head to look at him.

He looked relaxed in a way she still didn't completely trust—broad shoulders loose, jaw unclenched, the little lines at the corners of his eyes softer than when she'd first met him. It still surprised her sometimes that he could be this open, this unguarded, with her.

"You want to hear it?" she asked.

He rolled his head toward her, the corners of his mouth ghosting up. "Always."

She took a breath.

"I Am a Pure Being of Light and Love, guided by Source Creator at ALL times," she said, giving each capital letter its due like she'd been taught.

He let the words hang there for a moment.

"Bold," he said. "I like it."

"It feels... fake half the time," she admitted. "Like I'm LARPing as some healed, enlightened version of myself. I don't always feel pure, or light, or loving. A lot of days I feel like a burnt-out generator about to short-circuit."

"Maybe that's why you say it," he replied. "Not because it's descriptive. Because it's aspirational. A reminder."

"What's the opposite?" she asked.

He thought for a beat.

"'I am a broken being of fear and scarcity, guided by unresolved trauma at all times,'" he said.

She snorted. "Okay. That one fits most Mondays."

"Sure," he said. "But only part of you. Not the whole. I've met the other part. The light-and-love one. Even when you're cussing me out."

She eased down beside him, copying his posture: flat on her back, eyes on the stars. Their shoulders touched. The contact grounded her more than any app ever had.

"Do you ever feel silly?" she asked. "Two grown-ass people lying on a roof in Guatemala, talking about Source and guidance and... whatever the hell this is?"

"Constantly," he said. "Then I picture myself pretending not to care about any of it, and I like this version way better."

She exhaled slowly.

"Do you think we're crazy for doing this?" she asked. "No contract. No ring. Just... 'Hi, we've decided the universe has sanctioned our situationship, so we're committed now.'"

He turned his head toward her again.

"I think contracts can be sacred for some people," he said. "I think rings can be beautiful. I also think if we did that just to prove something to other people, this would feel like a costume."

"And right now?" she pressed.

"Right now, it feels like we stood in front of something bigger than paperwork and said, 'We choose this. Every damn day. Until we don't,'" he said. "That's scarier and more honest than any legal document I can think of."

She let that sit.

"I don't want a wedding," she said quietly. "I don't want a room full of people staring at me, waiting for me to be some polished, princess version of myself. I don't want to sign something and feel like I've just signed up to dissolve into it."

"I know," he said. "And I don't want that for you. Or for me. I just want what we're already doing, but better: chosen, not slipped into. Witnessed by whoever's listening up there."

He jerked his chin toward the stars.

"Source Creator?" she asked, teasing.

"And the TSA agent who keeps checking my passport every three months," he added. "They've definitely witnessed some things."

She laughed, the sound surprising her with how free it felt.

Silence stretched, but it wasn't the old, suffocating kind. More like two people sharing the same air without needing to fill it.

After a while, she said, "Miri's late."

He didn't pretend to misunderstand.

"Late late?" he asked.

"Yeah," she said. "Two weeks. She texted me this morning..."

Her thumb instinctively moved like she was scrolling back to the message.

"...She said she's trying not to panic. Trying not to Google."

"With Antonio," he said quietly.

She nodded.

The name sat between them like a small, ugly stone.

"Well," he said eventually, "that... complicates the map."

"Understatement of the year," she murmured.

She closed her eyes.

I Am a Pure Being of Light and Love, guided by Source Creator at ALL times....

"Guided," she whispered. "Then why does the guidance system keep sending in men like that at crucial plot points?"

A trumpet run floated up from somewhere below bright, then dissonant, then resolving.

"Ask Rashad," Zeke said. "He'll say something about jazz needing tension before release."

"Rashad would say life is a solo over a rhythm section you didn't choose," she said.

"Exactly," he replied. "And right now, Antonio is definitely the out-of-tune horn."

She laughed again, but her mind had already drifted:

To Miri in Houston, or maybe in her apartment in San Antonio, staring at a bathroom mirror.

To Antonio's butter-knife smile.

To the way the universe sometimes sent the same test in a new outfit.

She opened her eyes and stared at the stars harder.

If she was a Pure Being of Light and Love, guided at all times, then this next part—Miri, the scare, the way it would ripple through all of them—was part of that guidance, too.

She hated that.

But she knew it was true.

Chapter 2 – Storms on the Line

Miri didn't call the next day.

She texted.

Miri:

I took the test.

Reina's stomach tightened.

Reina:

And?

Dots appeared, disappeared, reappeared.

Miri:

Negative.

Reina let out a breath she hadn't noticed she'd been holding.

Reina:

Okay. How do you feel?

A longer pause this time.

Miri:

Relieved.

And... weirdly sad?

And mad at myself for even being in this position.

Reina chewed on her lip.

Reina:

Want to talk voice or are you not up for my Very Serious Therapist Tone?

Miri:

Give me 10. I gotta cry in the shower first.

Reina smiled sadly at the screen.

Zeke came out onto the rooftop again with two mugs of coffee, bare feet slapping the tiles. He handed her one and sat down cross-legged beside her.

"News?" he asked.

"Negative," she said. "But she's a mess."

"Of course she is," he said. "Fear and maybe-hope don't just switch off because a stick says one line instead of two."

"Look at you with the poetic framing," she said.

"I hang out with a jazz instructor," he said. "Rhythm and metaphor by osmosis."

She looked at him over her mug.

"When did you tell your uncle what you do?" she asked. "I mean—about us. This… no-paper marriage."

"I told him we're committed," he said simply. "That I wasn't asking for his blessing, but I'd like his advice and his music."

"And what did he say?" she asked.

Zeke smirked, mimicking Rashad's voice: "Marriage is a contract with the state. Commitment is a contract with your soul. Don't confuse one for the other, and don't talk to me about kids until you've survived a tour together."

She snorted. "That sounds like him."

"He likes you," Zeke said. "You know that, right?"

"He likes that I call you on your shit," she said.

"Same thing," he replied.

Her phone buzzed again.

Miri:

Ok. Call me.

But if I hang up mid-sob, pretend it was a Wi-Fi issue.

Reina's chest tightened in a different way now—protective, sister-like.

She stood.

"I'm gonna go downstairs," she said. "Walls are thin up here. I don't want to make her cry in front of the whole city."

"Tell her I'm here if she needs a dude's opinion she can ignore," Zeke said.

"I will," Reina said.

"And Rei?" he added.

She paused at the doorway.

"Yeah?"

"Remember you're a Pure Being of Light and Love, guided by Source or whatever," he said. "Not a crisis center. You don't have to fix this for her."

She rolled her eyes, but her throat prickled.

"I know," she said.

"I'm serious," he pressed. "Be sister, not savior."

She nodded once, then headed down the stairs.

—

Miri answered on the first ring.

"I feel stupid," she said without hello.

"You're not stupid," Reina said. "You're human. Hi, by the way."

"Hola, señora del cielo," Miri said, her voice thick. "How's Guatemala? Still all magical and healing and full of men who buy you banana bread?"

"Don't pivot to me," Reina said gently. "How are you?"

Miri sniffed.

"I don't know," she said. "I'm... relieved. I didn't want a baby. Not with him. Not now. But there was this tiny traitor part of me that was like... maybe this is the thing. You know? The big life shift. And now that it's not happening, I'm mad at myself for even wanting it for a second."

"What did he say?" Reina asked.

Miri scoffed. "I haven't told him."

Reina went quiet.

"You slept with a man who's woven into your friend's relationship, and you didn't tell him about a pregnancy scare?" she said softly. "That's a lot to carry alone."

"I know," Miri whispered. "I know. I just... I already feel like the villain in some story, and I haven't even done anything irreversible yet."

"You're not the villain," Reina said. "You're a woman who made a messy choice with a messy man. That's not unique, babe. That's Tuesday."

Miri laughed weakly.

"You still want him?" Reina asked, not accusing—just curious.

"No," Miri said immediately. Then, after a beat: "Yes. Or I want... the attention. The way he looked at me like I was the main event for five minutes. I hate that I liked that. I hate that he picked the exact crack in my armor and slid right in."

Reina leaned against the cool plaster wall of the stairwell; phone pressed to her ear.

"You're not wrong about that armor," she said. "He did, too. That's his talent. Seeing the crack. Making it bigger."

"I thought I was past that," Miri said. "Past being impressed by a dude in a nice shirt who knows his way around a soundbite."

Reina's chest ached for her.

"You're not past being human," she said. "None of us are."

Silence stretched, just the sound of both of them breathing on opposite sides of a continent.

“I don’t want to blow up your thing with Zeke,” Miri blurted. “That’s my worst fear. That I am the storm in your cielo.”

Reina closed her eyes.

“You’re not the storm,” she said. “Antonio is the storm. You’re the person who got caught in the rain without an umbrella.”

“It was my choice to stand there,” Miri said.

“Yeah,” Reina said. “It was. You stood in the rain. You got scared. You got out. That’s the part I’m focusing on.”

Miri let out a shuddering breath.

“I’m going to talk to Tasha,” she said finally. “And maybe… maybe to Zeke. At some point. Before it becomes some secret that rots.”

Reina’s chest tightened. “Are you sure?”

“No,” Miri said. “But I’m surer that secrets rot. I’ve seen enough of those.”

They stayed on the phone until the tears ran out. When they finally hung up, Reina climbed back up to the rooftop.

Zeke was still on his back, eyes closed, listening to the trumpet from below and tapping his fingers along to it on his chest.

“How’s our girl?” he asked.

“Not pregnant,” Reina said. “But not okay.”

“Give it time,” he said. “Storm just passed.”

Reina lay back down beside him.

"Do you ever think about kids?" she asked, staring up.

"Sure," he said. "Then I remember I can barely keep my plants alive and reconsider."

"I'm serious," she said.

"So am I," he replied. Then, after a beat: "I think about it more now. Not as some abstract 'I should procreate' thing. As if it happened, would we be okay? Would we be... us, plus someone small, or would we disappear into parenting and forget we're people?"

She considered that.

"I don't know if I want them," she said. "But I know I don't want them with anyone who feels like a storm."

"And me?" he asked quietly. "Do I feel like sky or storm?"

She smiled, small and real.

"Sky with occasional thunderstorms," she said.

"I'll take it," he replied.

They lay there a little longer, listening to the trumpet below and the soft hum of the city, two people who had finally stopped hiding their fears from each other, even if they hadn't yet figured out what to do with them.

When they finally went downstairs, it was for late-night dishes, shared silence that didn't feel heavy, and the familiar ache of knowing that soon there would be airports and time zones between them again.

—

A few weeks later, after flights and goodbyes and slipping back into Houston's thicker air, Zeke sat at his kitchen table with his notebook open and his phone face-down beside it.

The jazz station played low in the background—some late-night set Rashad had texted him to listen to—but his mind was half a continent away.

He picked up his pen.

The depth of my sadness is immeasurable and will never be known.

I have many around me, yet I always feel alone.

I keep a happy face. A peaceful space.

My mind is consumed by the absence of her face.

I speak to myself often and confess my pain.

I miss her so much. I pray for the rain.

However, sunshine remains.

Star Gazing with her in Guatemala is indescribable with words.

Star Gazing anywhere with her is absolute clarity.

The sounds of the crisp and clear nights.

The voice of Reina is the greatest sound I've ever heard.

My Chapina… my señorita…

This is a multiverse kind of love that transcends time, distance, and conscious vibrations.

I am vulnerable and I embrace it.

I don't fake it.

Being without her I simply can't take it....

He stared at the lines for a long moment, feeling a little ridiculous and very relieved.

Then he closed the notebook, slid it back onto the shelf, and turned his phone screen up again—just in case her name lit it.

Distance did what distance always does—it stretched time, sharpened longing, and made every reunion feel both overdue and sacred.

Chapter 3 – Reina del Cielo

They didn't plan to talk about the past that night. The deep past, the before we knew each other past.

It started with a song.

They were in Houston now, months later, lying on Rashad's living-room floor while he rifled through records.

"You two ever really listen to Kind of Blue?" Rashad asked, holding up the album like scripture.

"I thought that was jazz law," Reina said. "Is it allowed to say no?"

"It's more like jazz gravity," Rashad said. "You can ignore it, but it's still holding you down." He slid the record out of its sleeve, set it on the turntable. The needle dropped with a soft hiss.

The opening notes of "So What" floated out: bass, piano, that horn line like a question mark drawn in the air.

"This is classroom stuff for you, right?" Reina asked Zeke quietly.

"This is church for Rashad," Zeke replied.

They lay there on the rug, heads close to one another, feet pointed opposite directions like they were on a compass.

"You know what I love about this record?" Rashad said from his armchair. "Everyone thinks it's heaven. Floating. But listen—" He pointed mid-air, conducting. "Listen to the tension. The blue notes. Heaven is not just the pretty parts. It's the dissonance resolving."

Reina closed her eyes.

Heaven. Cielo.

She thought of the affirmation. She thought of the way Zeke looked at her sometimes, like she was the only star in the room.

"You know you're beautiful, right?" Zeke said suddenly, like the thought had just slipped out of his mouth without permission.

Her eyes flew open. "Don't start," she said, cheeks already warming.

"I'm not starting anything," he said. "I'm just stating facts. You're beautiful. And it's rude not to inform you."

She groaned, half-hiding her face with her hand.

"Stop it some more," she muttered, grinning despite herself.

He laughed. "That's not how that phrase works."

"It is now," she said, voice soft but playful. "I don't know how to take compliments like a normal person, so you get whatever this is."

"Noted," he said. "I'll keep saying them, you keep telling me to stop it some more, and eventually your brain will catch up."

She shook her head, but the line between her brows had eased.

"Do you ever feel like I'm putting too much on you?" she asked suddenly, still a little pink from the compliment.

Zeke turned his head. "In what way?"

"Reina del Cielo," she said. "Queening me up in your head. Like I'm some… guiding star, or whatever."

"I call you that because of nights like Antigua," he said. "Rooftops. You talking to the sky like it owes you answers."

“That doesn’t make me your heaven,” she said. “It makes me a woman who doesn’t like being left in the dark.”

He studied her.

“You think Reina del Cielo means I’m putting you on a pedestal,” he said.

“A little,” she admitted. “I mean… Queen of the Sky? That’s a lot to live up to. Some days I’m Reina del I Forgot to Send the Invoice. Reina del Didn’t Call My Dad Back. Reina del Anxiety Spiral at 3 a.m.”

He smiled at that soft and sad all at once.

“You can be all of those,” he said. “And still be my Reina del Cielo.”

She snorted. “You say that like I’m your religion.”

“You’re not my religion,” he said. “You’re my… orientation.”

She blinked. “My what?”

“The direction I check against,” he said. “When I’m lost, I look at what ‘us’ feels like and I ask, ‘Am I moving toward that, or away?’ That’s all Reina del Cielo means to me. Not halos. Not perfection. Just—when everything goes dark, I know where up is because of you.”

Her chest pulled tight.

“Damn,” she whispered. “You rehearsed that?”

“A little,” he said, unapologetic. “You keep poking at the nickname; I had to figure out why I was insisting on it.”

She rolled onto her side to face him fully.

“I grew up with a very Catholic grandmother,” she said. “Cielo was this unreachable place where good girls went if they behaved and shut up about their needs. I'm allergic to that version of heaven. I don't want to be your Virgen de Guadalupe."

"I don't want you to be," he said quickly. "My heaven isn't 'up there,' it's… here. Us. This." He tapped the worn rug, then his chest. "The fact that we can fight and still stay. That we can tell the truth and not shatter. That's cielo to me."

She searched his face, looking for any trace of worship that would make her want to run.

Instead, she found something scarier: respect. And choice.

"How long have you been following me around, then?" she asked, lighter. "If I've been your orientation."

"Well," he said, "apparently since at least 2017."

She frowned. "What happened in 2017?"

"Austin," he said. "Staff well-being conference. Our hospital sent three of us. I almost didn't go. I thought it was going to be corporate fluff. Then the keynote speaker got up there and started talking about how 'your job will replace you before the obituary hits the paper.'"

Her heart stuttered.

"That was you," he said.

"I said that," she murmured.

He nodded. "You were in this ugly navy blazer and shoes that hurt your feet."

"Those damn shoes," she muttered automatically.

“The mic kept cutting out,” he went on. “You cursed under your breath in Spanish once when it did, thought the room couldn’t hear. I was in the third row, taking notes like my life depended on it.”

She stared at him, then let out a short, disbelieving laugh.

“No,” she said. “No way.”

“Yes way,” he said. “I still have the notebook. You scribbled something on the screen about ‘you are not your output’ and I wrote it down and then ignored it for three more years.”

She lay back, brain buzzing.

“We were in the same room,” she said.

“Yep,” he said. “You were burning out onstage. I was burning out in the audience.”

She threw an arm over her eyes.

“That’s messed up,” she said.

“Or perfect,” he said. “Depending how dramatic you’re feeling.”

“How many other times?” she asked.

“Music festival in ’04,” he said. “You remember the one in San Antonio? The year it poured, and everyone pretended mud was a personality?”

She groaned. “I still have those boots.”

“I was there,” he said. “Antonio dragged me. We left early because he got mad that some girl chose a drummer over him. You?”

“Stayed,” she said. “With my ex. We fought in the car on the way home about nothing and everything. You might’ve been the car next to us at that gas station off I-35.”

He laughed. “Wouldn’t surprise me.”

She was quiet for a long moment.

“So, I’ve been… overhead,” she said softly. “Your Reina del Cielo. In rooms you didn’t know how to name me in yet.”

He reached over and laced their fingers together.

“We’ve been each other’s background stars for a while,” he said. “Now we’re front and center. That’s the only difference.”

She let that image sink in not a goddess on a cloud, not an untouchable icon, just a star someone finally looked directly at.

“It still scares me,” she said. “Being that important to someone.”

“Me too,” he admitted. “Let’s be scared together.”

She turned their joined hands over, tracing the lines in his palm like a map.

“Don’t ever let ‘Reina del Cielo’ mean I can’t be human,” she said. “Promise me that.”

“I promise to call you Reina del Cielo when you’re crying and when you’re cussing and when you’re ignoring my texts,” he said. “Not because I need you to be better, but because I see who you are underneath all of it.”

Her eyes were stung.

“You’re really not going to marry me, are you,” she said, half-tease, half-test.

“No,” he said calmly. “Not in the state-sanctioned, white-dress way. Unless one day you wake up and you want that. Then we’ll revisit. But I’m not asking for it. I already have what I want.”

“And what’s that?” she whispered.

“You,” he said. “As you are. As you’re becoming. Reina of this sky and this mess. That’s enough for me. More than enough.”

Somewhere behind them, Rashad flipped the record and put the needle down again. A new track began—something softer, almost tender.

“Long live the queen,” Rashad said from his chair without looking over.

Reina laughed, wiping at her cheeks.

“Don’t encourage him,” she called.

“It’s already done,” Rashad said. “You’re in the liner notes now.”

She didn’t know if she believed in past lives, or soul contracts, or any of the things people on her podcasts talked about. But lying there with Zeke’s hand in hers, Miles in the speakers, and Rashad muttering about blue notes, she felt something settle.

Maybe cielo wasn’t a place.

Maybe it was a relationship you were finally safe inside.

Storms never travel alone. Even when they begin with two people, they move through everyone standing close enough to feel the weather change.

Chapter 4 – Weather Reports

The next time Miri visited Houston, the air between her and Antonio felt different.

The scare had come and gone. The test had read negative. She cried, journaled, apologized to herself quietly. She'd told Tasha. She had not told Zeke—not yet. The thought of seeing the disappointment in his eyes kept shoving that confession into the "later" folder.

At Zeke's place, the four of them—Zeke, Reina, Miri, Tasha—waited for Antonio to show.

"I can cancel," Reina had offered.

"No," Miri had said. "Storms don't disappear because you close the windows. They find another way in. I'd rather see him in daylight with reinforcements."

When Antonio finally walked in, arms full of beer and easy charm, Miri's pulse jumped in that traitorous way she hated.

"Ladies," he said, kissing the air near their cheeks. "Zeke. My emotional support jazz uncle."

"Don't claim me," Rashad called from the kitchen. "I'm deniability only."

They laughed.

Later, Miri found herself alone in the hallway with Antonio while everyone else argued over a playlist.

"You good?" he asked.

"Yeah," she lied.

He gave her a longer look. "You've been quiet."

"I'm allowed," she said. "I'm processing."

"Processing what?" he asked, lowering his voice. "Us?"

"There is no us," she shot back, maybe too fast.

He smiled, slow and knowing. "Sure."

For a heartbeat, the hall narrowed, the noise from the living room dimmed, and it was just them and the too-bright fact of what they'd done.

Then Tasha's voice floated down the hall, sharp and saving.

"Hey, Miri," she said. "Reina needs you in here before she throws Zeke's phone out the window for playing the wrong version of 'Creep.'"

Miri didn't look away from Antonio as she answered.

"Coming," she said.

She stepped around him, careful not to touch him.

In the living room, Reina handed her a drink without comment.

"You, okay?" Reina murmured.

"I will be," Miri said. "He's weather. I'm bringing my own umbrella next time."

Reina bumped into her shoulder.

"There's my girl," she said.

What had once felt too heavy to carry slowly became something else in Reina's hands. Not lighter, exactly. Just more honest. More hers.

Chapter 5 – Queen of the Sky, Queen of the Mess

Weeks later, back in Guatemala, Reina stood alone on that same rooftop where she'd started her affirmation practice.

The stars were out in full—scattershot and indifferent.

She closed her eyes.

"I Am a Pure Being of Light and Love, guided by Source Creator at ALL times," she whispered.

The words didn't feel like a costume as much anymore. They felt like a direction. Like the "north" on a compass, even when she was wandering.

Behind her, footsteps padded softly across the tiles.

"Talking to yourself again?" Zeke asked.

"Talking to Source," she said. "And to the part of me that still wants to run."

He slid his arms around her from behind, chin resting on her shoulder.

"How's she doing tonight?" he asked. "The runner."

"Tired," Reina said. "Less... sprint. More like power walking"

"Good," he murmured.

They looked up together.

“Hey, Reina del Cielo,” he said softly. “What’s the forecast up there?”

She smiled.

“Clear,” she said. “With a chance of miracles.”

“And down here?” he asked, giving her a gentle squeeze.

She thought of her dad, still alive, managing his meds. Of Miri, choosing better questions for herself after a storm. Of Tasha, sending voice notes that sounded like love disguised as sarcasm. Of Rashad, writing her name in his mental liner notes.

Of Zeke, who had once been a stranger in a café and was now the one person she trusted with both her sky and her weather.

“Partly messy,” she said. “But I think... I’ve finally got the right co-pilot.”

He kissed the side of her neck.

“Long live the queen,” he said again, almost a whisper.

“For however long Source Creator sanctions this madness,” she replied.

They stood there, two not-married, deeply committed, slightly ridiculous humans under a sky that had watched them almost meet a dozen times before they finally looked up at the same time.

Reina took a breath.

She didn’t feel perfect.

She felt present.

For the first time, “Reina del Cielo” didn’t sound like an impossible role somebody had cast her in.

It sounded like the name of the woman she was in the process of becoming queen of her own inner sky, queen of this messy, miracle-filled little heaven they were building together.

And that, she decided, had real merit.

Story Three – STOP IT SOME MORE

"Covenant above contract. Playlist above paperwork. One roof, two roots, same sky."

Previously, in "REINA DEL CIELO" ...

Reina Delgado and Zeke Ali took their love out of the café and into the real world—rooftops in Guatemala, long-distance phone calls, and hard conversations in Houston living rooms. Reina wrestled with being "Reina del Cielo," not as a saint on a pedestal, but as the compass of Zeke's heart. Zeke learned to say what he felt without a contract to hide behind.

They watched Miri survive a pregnancy scare with Antonio, saw Tasha step into a healthier career, and listened as Uncle Rashad played his horn and told the truth about regret and real heaven. Between affirmations, blue notes, and honest fear, they chose each other again—no rings, no paperwork, just a daily, deliberate yes.

Now, in "Stop It Some More," they must decide what it really means to share not just a love, but a life: one roof in Guatemala, roots in Houston, a soundtrack of Natiruts and MC Magic, and a future that refuses to fit anyone else's script.

Chapter 1 – Precious Alignment

The first thing Reina noticed when she woke up was the light.

Not the harsh, alarm-clock light of her old life—phone screen glow, fluorescent office, the blue-white of too-early emails—but the soft, sideways gold of a Guatemalan morning pushing through thin curtains.

The second thing she noticed was Zeke's hand on her stomach.

Heavy, warm, spread wide like he was holding down the center of the world.

His breath ghosted across the back of her neck, slow and steady. The ceiling fan hummed its lazy circle above them. Outside, someone pushed a cart down the cobblestone street, the squeak-thump of wheels and footsteps a rhythm she'd come to associate with a kind of peace.

She eased onto her back to look at him.

He was still mostly asleep, lips parted just enough to be a little undignified. His dreads were smashed on one side, the faintest smudge of pillow crease on his cheek. Forty-something and soft in the ways she'd come to adore: laugh lines, a tiny scar by his eyebrow from some long-ago hospital mishap, the way his face relaxed completely when he felt safe.

“You’re staring,” he murmured, eyes still closed.

“You’re snoring,” she countered.

“I don’t snore,” he said, opening one eye.

“You snore like a gentle old dog,” she said. “It’s endearing.”

“Endearing,” he repeated. “I’ll put that on my dating profile.”

She glared.

He grinned. “Kidding. Calm down. My dating profile has been deactivated by the Universe.”

“Good,” she said. “Source Creator has taste.”

He shifted onto his side, propping his head on his hand so he could really look at her. Morning made him softer, somehow. Less defense, more truth.

“You know you’re beautiful, right?” he said.

There it was.

She groaned, rolling her eyes, but the warmth that rushed to her face gave her away.

“Don’t start,” she muttered.

“I’m not starting,” he said. “I’m continuing a well-established fact. You’re beautiful in the morning. You’re beautiful when you’re annoyed. You’re beautiful when you’re cussing out your laptop. It’s very consistent.”

She buried her face in the pillow for a second, smiling where he couldn't see.

"Stop it some more," she mumbled into the cotton.

Zeke laughed, the sound low and happy.

"There it is," he said. "My favorite wrong phrase."

She peeked up at him. "It's not wrong. It's... advanced English."

"Is that what we're calling it?" he asked.

"Yes," she said. "It means 'I can't handle your compliments but secretly I can, so please proceed with caution.'"

He traced a lazy circle on her stomach with his thumb.

"Duly noted," he said. "I'll proceed with extreme, relentless caution."

She shook her head but didn't bat his hand away.

There was a time, not that long ago, when waking up like this would've made her skin itch. Not because of him specifically, but because of the implications. Shared space, shared mornings, shared futures. All of the ways people could fail each other after lying in exactly this kind of light, making exactly this kind of promise with their bodies and not their words.

Now, the itch was smaller. A manageable tingle instead of a full-body rash.

She exhaled.

"So," she said, "how does it feel to finally be in 'precious alignment' with your queen of the sky?"

He snorted. "Did you just quote my uncle at me?"

"He texted me yesterday," she said, reaching over to grab her phone from the nightstand. "Sent me this long, dramatic message about how 'when your head, heart, feet, and beat line up, that's precious alignment, niña.'"

Zeke laughed. "That sounds exactly like him."

"He said we're in a 'rare pocket of alignment' right now," she went on. "That we should enjoy it before life throws the next plot twist."

"That man cannot just let us be happy," Zeke said. "There always has to be a lesson."

"He's not wrong, though," she said.

They lay there for a moment, listening to the quiet.

It was a rare pocket.

For the first time since they'd decided to try this thing for real, there were no imminent flights booked, no hospital crises, no looming deadlines on contracts or grants. Zeke had taken two full weeks off—really off, not "checking email in between tourist photos" off—and flown down. Reina had cleared her calendar except for a few check-ins. Her dad's latest test results had been steady. Miri saw someone new who actually texted back in complete sentences. Antonio had, blessedly, gone largely silent.

Everything, improbably, was... okay.

"Do you trust it?" he asked quietly.

She didn't pretend not to understand.

"This?" she asked, gesturing vaguely between them, at the room, the morning. "Or... all of it?"

"All of it," he said.

She thought about that.

Her old reflex was no. Of course not. Trust was how you got blindsided. Trust was the first step on the road to waking up at 3 a.m. wondering how you'd become a stranger in your own life.

But something had shifted since Antigua, since Houston, since rooftop confessions and living-room jazz sermons.

"I'm learning to," she said finally. "To trust that we're not going to bail the second it's not easy. To trust that I'm not going to bail the second I feel weird."

"You used to bail in your head before people even knew there was a problem," he said gently.

"I still do," she admitted. "But now I text you first."

He smiled. "Progress."

She watched his face, the way his eyes crinkled slightly at the corners when he was really seeing her, not just hearing her.

"Do you ever think we're... too old for this?" she asked. "For this level of drama and flights and spiritual affirmations and jazz lectures?"

He raised an eyebrow. "You want to go back to being numb in a job you hated?"

"No," she said immediately.

"Then no," he replied. "We're exactly old enough to know this is better."

She let out a breath she didn't know she'd been holding.

"Precious alignment," she said. "I kind of hate how much I like that phrase."

"You like it because it sounds like astrology and therapy had a baby," he said.

She laughed. "Shut up."

He brushed a curl back from her forehead.

"Head, heart, feet, and beat," he said. "That's what Rashad told me once. 'Head' is your thoughts. 'Heart' is your feelings. 'Feet' is what you do. 'Beat' is the rhythm of your life, the habits, the music you move to. When they all line up… you have a precious alignment. Most folks never get there on purpose. They stumble into it or miss it completely."

"And you think we're there?" she asked, suspicious and hopeful at the same time.

"I think we're closer than we've ever been," he said. "We want each other in our heads, we feel it in our hearts, our feet keep walking back to the same places—Houston, Guatemala, that stupid café—and our beat is slowly syncing up."

She made a face. "Did you just say our beat is syncing up?"

"I did," he said. "I regret nothing."

She slid a leg over his hip, pulling herself closer.

"What if the alignment doesn't last?" she asked quietly, voice muffled against his chest now. "What if this is a fluke?"

"Then we enjoy the hell out of the fluke," he said. "And when the next misalignment comes, we remember we had this. That we can get back to it. That's the difference. Before, we didn't even know what this felt like."

She let that wash over her.

He was right.

She'd had good moments in her marriage, in old jobs, in old flings. But they'd always felt separately like islands you swam to and then left, never fully part of the mainland of her life.

This felt... integrated. Like the same person who answered client emails and changed her dad's pillbox and made grocery lists was the one who lay here, being ridiculous about stars and affirmations and a man who wouldn't stop calling her queen.

"I still reserve the right to freak out sometimes," she said.

"Of course," he said. "I reserve the right to overthink and send you three-paragraph texts about nothing."

"You already do that," she said.

"I know," he replied. "Precious alignment doesn't mean we stop being ourselves. It just means we point all our weirdness in the same direction."

She smiled against his chest.

"Okay, Mr. Orientation," she said. "Say one more nice thing and then I'm cutting you off for the morning."

He pretended to think.

"Your laugh is my favorite sound," he said finally. "Even when it's at my expense. Especially then."

Her whole body became a little soft.

"Stop it some more," she said.

This time, she didn't bury her face. She let him see the way the words made her eyes shine, the way her mouth tilted up like it couldn't help itself.

"Gladly," he said.

He kissed her forehead, then her nose, then the corner of her mouth.

Down in the street, the cart's squeak-thump moved on. The city woke up.

Up here, for a moment, everything lined up: head, heart, feet, and beat. Two people who had spent most of their lives out of sync with themselves and everyone else, lying in a shaft of soft gold light, choosing—again—to believe they deserved this.

Precious alignment.

She decided she could live with that phrase.

At least for now.

Morning has a way of making promises feel easy. By afternoon, life usually wants details.

Chapter 2 – One Life, Two Places

By the time the coffee cooled, the emails had ruined the mood.

Reina watched Zeke's face change in real time as he scrolled through his inbox on his phone—forehead tightening, mouth settling into that thin line he wore in meetings.

"Uh-oh," she said. "Your eyebrows just clocked into work."

He huffed out a laugh, still reading.

"Remember that expansion project I consulted on last year?" he asked. "The new wing at the main hospital?"

"The one with the nightmare plumbing?" she said. "Yes. I remember the cursing."

"They want me to come on as 'Director of Infrastructure Strategy," he said, finger tracing the screen. "Full-time. Benefits. Budget authority. All the grown-man bells and whistles."

She sat up a little straighter.

"That sounds... big," she said carefully.

"It is," he said. "And it's the first time they've offered me something like this instead of just another contract."

He set the phone down, staring at it like it might explode.

"And?" she prompted.

“And it would mean I need to be in Houston most of the year,” he said. “Meetings. Site visits. Being the guy in the room, not the voice on the video call.”

She felt the little pocket of morning peace tighten.

“Did you... want that?” she asked.

“Ten years ago?” he said. “I would’ve sold my soul for it. Now?” He blew out his breath. “Now I have to measure it against... this.”

He gestured around them—the little bedroom in Antigua, the faint volcano outline through the window, her slippers on the floor next to his shoes.

Her phone buzzed on the nightstand like it had been waiting for its cue.

She picked it up.

Subject: Proposal – Long-Term Staff Wellbeing Program

Sender: Centro de Salud San Rafael

She scanned quickly.

“Hmm,” she said.

“‘Hmm’ what?” he asked.

“Remember that clinic I did a one-off workshop for?” she said. “They want to build a full program. Two years. They’re asking if I can base myself here for at least nine months out of the year while we roll it out.”

They both stared at their respective screens for a moment, then at each other.

“Well,” Zeke said. “That’s... symmetrical.”

"Cruel," she corrected. "But yes. Symmetrical."

Silence stretched, full of math and maps and old fears.

"Okay," he said finally. "So… what are our options that don't involve one of us disappearing into the other's life?"

She exhaled. "You go first."

"We could both say no," he said slowly. "Stay exactly how we are now. Keep… floating."

"And spend the next ten years wondering what would've happened if we'd been brave?" she said. "Pass."

"We could pick one city and force the other to pretend they're fine," he said.

"We've both tried that," she replied. "Different people. Different cities. Same disaster."

He nodded.

"Or" he said, "we could be honest about what we already know."

"Which is?" she asked.

"You breathe better here," he said. "In this air. In this language. In this work. Every time you land in Guatemala, your shoulders drop two inches."

Her throat tightened.

"And you?" she asked.

"I matter there," he said. "In Houston. Those hospitals, those systems—they're my instrument. But I don't need to be there 365 days a year to keep playing. I can structure it. Projects. Blocks of time. I just… never thought I could."

"Until now," she said quietly.

"Until now," he agreed.

They sat with that, no one offering to martyr themselves, no one pretending to be fine living in a life that didn't fit.

"Let's not decide from fear," she said. "Not this time. Not 'what's safest,' but 'what's truest.'"

"Truest is you in Guatemala," he said. "And me… finding a way to orbit that without losing my own gravity."

"You really think you could do that?" she asked. "Travel in for projects, not live in the hospital full-time?"

"If I'm brave? Yeah," he said. "If you're here waiting when I land."

She swallowed.

"I can be here," she said. "If 'here' is ours. Not just my escape hatch."

He smiled, small but real.

"Then we ask Rashad how to play this hand," he said. "Because it's not the one either of us thought we'd get."

"Head and heart are leaning Guatemala," she said. "Feet and beat need a coach."

"Exactly," he replied.

—

They didn't bring it up again until they were on the plane.

Two weeks later, the volcanoes of Guatemala shrank into the clouds beneath them. Reina leaned her head against the window, watching the patchwork of green and stone fade.

"Leaving still hurts," she said softly.

"It means it mattered," Zeke replied.

She glanced at him. "You sure you want to burn one of your precious vacation windows going back to Houston instead of sneaking off somewhere new with me?"

"My mom would kill me if she found out I was in the States and didn't show my face," he said. "And your dad's cardiologist appointment is next week. And Rashad's got that jam session with Jalen. Feels like the universe scheduled a family meeting."

She huffed a small laugh. "You just want Uncle Rashad to solve our life with a metaphor."

"Obviously," he said. "Head, heart, feet, beat. We talked about the first two on that roof. Time to consult the rhythm section."

She let her eyes close for a moment, the hum of the engines wrapping around her.

Houston meant:

Her dad's steady breaths in a recliner.

Her mom's questions were half worry, half gossip.

Rashad's chalk-dust stories and sax riffs.

Zeke in his element at the hospital.

Guatemala meant:

Thin, bright air.

Spanish rolling off her tongue.

Clients who saw her as a bridge.

Rooftops and stars and mornings like the one they'd just had.

"Two places, one life," she murmured.

"What was that?" he asked.

"Nothing," she said. "Just... rehearsing."

"For what?"

"For telling your uncle we want to live in both," she said. "And not sound completely out of our minds."

He squeezed her hand.

"He's a jazz instructor," Zeke said. "He spends his whole life teaching people how to live in between notes. If anyone gets it, he will."

The captain's voice crackled overhead, announcing their descent into Houston.

Reina took a breath.

Guatemala in her lungs.

Houston on the horizon.

Rashad's voice waiting somewhere on the other end of baggage claim, ready to turn their chaos into a lesson.

"Okay," she said. "Let's go play the hand we have."

Chapter 3 – Playing the Hand

The club was smaller than Zeke expected.

When Rashad had said, "They're inviting me to sit in at Blue Lamp," Zeke had pictured something with a marquee, a line down the block, velvet ropes. Instead, Blue Lamp was a narrow room tucked between a laundromat and a pawn shop—brick walls, a tiny stage, mismatched tables, and a bar that looked older than all three of them put together.

It was perfect.

"You nervous?" Zeke asked, as they stood in the doorway.

Rashad snorted, adjusting his glasses. "At my age? I'm nervous about stairs and cholesterol. Not about twelve bars in B-flat."

"You know what I mean," Zeke said. "This is a big deal, Unc. Jam session with Jalen Price. You've been talking about his records since I was a kid."

"Jalen's just a man with a horn," Rashad said. "Talented, yes. One kidney, bad knees, two divorces—just like the rest of us."

Zeke laughed.

They slid into a small table near the stage. Reina sat on Zeke's other side, fingers wrapped around a club soda, taking in the room.

"You sure you don't want a drink?" Zeke asked Rashad.

"I'm teaching tomorrow at 8 a.m.," Rashad said. "Can't show up to class smelling like regret."

"Your students would probably think it's cologne," Reina said.

“Jazz Funk by Regret,” Rashad mused. “Top notes of cigarette smoke and missed opportunities. I’ll pass.”

The house trio started with the piano, bass, drums, easing the crowd into something mid-tempo and bluesy. People talked softly, the clink of glass and murmur of voices filling the spaces between notes.

Halfway through the second tune, Jalen Price walked in.

He was shorter than his album covers made him look, gray at the temples, trumpet case in hand. He nodded to a few people, exchanged quick hugs, then his eyes landed on Rashad.

“Professor Rashad,” Jalen said, coming over. “You made it.”

Rashad stood, shaking his hand. “You keep putting out records, I keep showing up. Law of the universe.”

Jalen grinned, then looked past him to Zeke and Reina. “These your people?”

“This is my nephew Zeke,” Rashad said. “And his… complicated, universe-sanctioned situation, Reina.”

Reina extended her hand. “I prefer ‘partner.’”

“Partner works,” Jalen said, shaking it. “You good, partner?”

She smiled. “Working on it.”

“Always,” Jalen said. He turned back to Rashad. “You ready to sit in?”

Rashad spread his hands. “You really want an old head crashing your set?”

“I want the man who taught half my students how to hear a blue note,” Jalen said. “Come on.”

They headed up to the stage.

Zeke watched Rashad pick up a battered alto sax from its case like it was made of glass and memory. He adjusted the neck strap, tested the reed, then nodded to Jalen.

The pianist counted off.

The tune was "Footprints," something modal and loose. Jalen took the head, his trumpet line clean and bright, then handed it off with a glance.

Rashad stepped in.

His sound was different—rounder, smokier. Less about showing off, more about saying something. He bent notes, leaned into dissonance, then brought it back home in a way that made the tiny hairs on Zeke's arms stand up.

Reina leaned in close and whispered, "Your uncle is not playing."

"He never has," Zeke murmured.

When the tune ended, the applause felt bigger than the room.

After a couple more songs, there was a break. Musicians milled around the bar, wiping sweat, laughing, trading stories.

Rashad came back to the table, cheeks flushed, eyes brighter than Zeke had seen in years.

"You killed it," Zeke said.

"I didn't die," Rashad said. "That's enough."

"Stop it some more," Reina told him, grinning.

Rashad chuckled. "I see the phrase is spreading."

Jalen walked over, trumpet case back in his hand.

“You still got it,” he told Rashad. “Maybe more than before.”

“I got mileage,” Rashad said. “Skill plus mileage equals seasoning. Young cats don’t like hearing that.”

Jalen laughed, shook his head. “You always drop a proverb when a compliment shows up.”

“That’s how I deflect,” Rashad said. “I’m emotionally constipated.”

They all laughed.

After a moment, Jalen’s face grew more thoughtful.

“You know,” he said, “I used to wish I’d come up in New York in the ’50s. All my heroes, all those scenes. Thought if I’d just been born in the right time, right place, I’d be somebody different by now.”

Rashad nodded. “Yeah. I used to wish I’d been born with your horn instead of this little school sax.”

Jalen looked at him. “You’re serious?”

“I teach at a community college, Jalen,” Rashad said. “Most days it’s me and eighteen-year-olds who think Coltrane is a sneaker brand. You don’t think there were nights I laid awake thinking, ‘If I’d just moved, if I’d just hustled harder, maybe I’d have been the one on those records instead of in that classroom.”

Zeke felt something tightening in his chest. He’d never heard Rashad say that out loud.

“But here’s the thing,” Rashad went on, tapping the table for emphasis. “We don’t get to play the hand we wish we had. We have to play the hand we got.”

He looked at Zeke, then at Reina, then back at Jalen.

“And that hand?” he said. “It’s still music. Maybe I didn’t tour the world. But those kids in my class? They’re out there playing right now because some old fool with a chalkboard told them a diminished scale could be a prayer. That’s my lane. That’s my stage.”

Jalen’s jaw flexed.

“Be the best at whatever it is you do,” Rashad said. “And good at. Not the thing you fantasize about. The thing that’s in front of you. That’s where the real stuff happens.”

Zeke swallowed.

Reina blinked a couple of times like she was bookmarking the words.

Jalen let out a long breath. “You always did preach better than any church I’ve been in,” he said. “For what it’s worth, those kids talk about you like you’re the Miles of that campus.”

Rashad waved a hand, embarrassed. “Stop it some more,” he muttered.

Reina laughed. “See? Advanced English.”

Jalen checked his watch. “We’re about to start the next set,” he said. “You want in on a ballad?”

“Nah,” Rashad said. “I got what I came for. You young cats take it from here. I gotta be coherent at 8 a.m.”

Jalen clasped his shoulder. “Thank you,” he said simply.

After he left, they sat in a little bubble of quiet at the table.

“You really wanted the other hand that bad?” Zeke asked.

"Of course," Rashad said. "I'm human. I wanted the poster, the tour, and the liner notes with my name big. But wanting ain't the same as being called to it."

He looked at his nephew.

"You the same," he said. "You could've chased titles instead of systems. Reina could've chased status instead of sanity. Miri could've chased the storm instead of doing the hard work of getting dry. Antonio—" He stopped, shook his head. "Antonio still out here trying to bluff with a busted hand."

Reina snorted. "You're not wrong."

Rashad leaned back, watching Jalen step onto the stage again.

"You two," he said, nodding at Zeke and Reina, "you got a weird little hand. Two cities, too much history, a lot of therapy, one annoying uncle. But it's yours. Play it the best way you can. That's all any of us get."

Zeke felt something in him unclench.

All the questions about where to live, how to split their time, whether they were "doing life right" shifted slightly.

Not gone—just... reframed.

"It feels... small sometimes," Reina admitted. "This life. Compared to what I thought I'd have."

"It only feels small when you're comparing it to somebody else's stage," Rashad said. "From where I'm sitting? A woman who gets to do work she believes in, split her time between two places she loves, and wake up next to a man who actually shows up? That's not small. That's rare."

She looked down, fighting with a smile.

“Stop it some more,” she said softly.

Rashad chuckled. “See? Advanced English.”

Zeke reached for her hand under the table and squeezed.

Precious alignment, he thought.

Not perfect.

But exact for them.

And in that dim little club, with a jazz legend back onstage and his uncle quietly glowing in the half-light, he understood Rashad’s lesson in a new way:

They didn’t need a different hand.

They just needed to keep playing this one—with all the heart they had.

They left Blue Lamp with the strange calm that comes after hearing the truth said out loud. Nothing in their lives was suddenly simpler. But it had become harder to lie to themselves about what they wanted.

Chapter 4 – One Roof, Two Roots

They didn't talk about it in the car.

On the drive back from Blue Lamp, Rashad hummed along to something on the jazz station, tapping the steering wheel in soft, syncopated patterns. Zeke stared out the window, neon blurring into darkness. Reina watched the city roll past—the strip malls, the late-night taquerías, the clusters of oak trees holding down the horizon.

Houston was in her bones. So was leaving it.

At Rashad's house, there were hugs and leftover cake and promises to "call when you land next time." Diesel's future chew toy—though neither of them knew it yet—was still on the windowsill, waiting for its destiny.

Later, back at Zeke's mom's place, they slipped into the small guest room that had seen them through more transitions than it deserved.

Reina kicked off her sandals and sat cross-legged on the bed. Zeke closed the door, leaned against it, hands in his pockets like a man about to testify.

"So," she said.

"So," he echoed.

The word hung there, full of everything Rashad had just said about hands and stages and being the best at what you do.

Reina took a breath.

“I want to live in Guatemala,” she said.

There. Out loud.

No hedging. No softening.

“I know,” he said.

That stopped her.

“You do?” she asked.

“Head and heart have been screaming it for a while,” he said. “Feet have just been catching up.”

She looked at him, searching for resentment and not finding it.

“You don’t feel like I’m dragging you away from your life?” she asked.

He pushed off the door, came to sit beside her on the bed.

“You are my life,” he said simply. “Houston is my work. My family. My people. That doesn’t go away because I change my address. It just means I travel to it instead of waking up in it.”

“Travel is expensive,” she said automatically.

“Regret is more expensive,” he said. “We just heard that from a man who could’ve chased New York in the ’50s and instead chose a classroom in Houston in the 2000s.”

She smiled despite herself.

“True,” she said.

“I don’t want to be eighty in this guest room thinking, ‘I could’ve woken up in Guatemala half my life and I chose not to because I was scared of changing my mailing address,’” he said.

She laughed softly. “When you put it like that…”

He reached for her hand.

"I need Houston," he said. "But I don't need it every day. I can structure my consulting so I'm there for stretches. Big projects. Audits. Training. I'll have to have some hard conversations, but they already fly people in for less. I'm valuable. I can negotiate."

"Talk your talk," she said, a little impressed.

"And you," he said, "need Guatemala. Not as a vacation, but as home. Your work hums there. Your body relaxes. Your Spanish is stupidly good."

"I do love being able to swear properly," she admitted.

He squeezed her fingers.

"So, we make Guatemala home," he said. "Get a place. A real one. With our stuff in it. Not just a borrowed apartment or an Airbnb. Then I build my work around that center of gravity. Houston becomes my orbit, not my anchor."

"And my parents?" she asked quietly. "Your mom? We can't just... vanish."

"We won't," he said. "We plan blocks. Months here. Video calls that aren't just check-ins but real talks. Bring them down when we can. Bring Guatemala to them in little ways when we can't. Two roots. One roof."

She rolled the phrase around in her head.

"One roof, two roots," she repeated. "I like that. Sounds like something your uncle would write on a whiteboard and then riff about for twenty minutes."

"Head, heart, feet, beat," he said. "Head and heart say: home is where we both feel most alive. Feet can walk between. Beat can adapt."

She let out a breath she didn't know she'd been holding.

"I was afraid to say it," she admitted. "Afraid you'd hear 'Guatemala' and think 'she doesn't want my world.'"

"I did, a little," he confessed. "At first. But then I watched you here. In Houston. You show up. You take care of my mom. You sit through my long stories about boiler valves. You are not running from this place. You're just not meant to be trapped in it."

"And you're not meant to be trapped in Antigua either," she said. "You'd go nuts if you couldn't go crawl around a mechanical room every few months."

"True," he said. "I like my boilers."

She groaned. "That's the least sexy sentence I've ever heard."

"You say that now," he said. "Wait until you see me negotiate a chiller replacement remotely."

She shoved his shoulder, laughing.

"Okay," she said, sobering a little. "So... practically. We find a place in Antigua. Long-term. We make it ours."

"A real roof," he said. "Our bed. Our cups. Our socks in the same drawer."

"Gross," she said, but her eyes were bright.

"I restructure with the hospital," he went on. "Pitch them on a consultant model that includes a certain number of on-site months. We batch your Houston family time into those windows, so we're not ping-ponging constantly."

"And I plan my clinic work and org contracts around being there most of the year," she said. "If I need to travel for a project, we talk about it like we do everything else now. No solo decisions based on panic."

"No panic moves," he agreed. "Only star-aligned moves."

She let that shift inside her for a second.

"Are we really ready for this?" she asked. "Like—really moving? Not just visiting. Not just 'I'll see you in three months.' Actually... one roof?"

He tilted her chin up, so she was looking at him.

"We've already done the hard part," he said. "We chose each other. We told the truth. We didn't bail when it got scary. A roof is just... geography catching up to what our hearts already decided."

She blinked back a sudden rush of tears.

"You're getting good at this," she said. "You know that?"

"Stop it some more," he murmured.

She laughed, wiping at one eye.

"Okay," she said. "One roof."

"Two roots," he replied.

"Guatemala for the roof," she said. "Houston for the roots."

"And stars connecting both," he added.

He leaned in, pressed his forehead to hers.

"Star gazing in Guatemala," he said. "Literally now. Not just metaphor."

She smiled into the almost-kiss.

“Then we better get used to MC Magic echoing off those walls,” she said. “Because if I’m living there full-time, he’s on the playlist.”

He groaned. “Of course he is.”

She smirked.

“You realize my teenage dream was to slow dance in my own place to MC Magic with a man who actually knew my middle name,” she said. “You might as well lean in.”

“What is your middle name?” he asked, teasing.

She swatted his chest. “Too late. You have already signed the cosmic contract. No refunds.”

He laughed.

“One roof,” he said again.

“Two roots,” she replied.

And for the first time, instead of feeling like a choice between lives, it felt like the only way their one, wild, shared life could ever really fit.

In the weeks that followed, what had sounded wild in a guest room in Houston slowly became practical. Phone calls were made. Contracts were reshaped. Suitcases were packed with more certainty than fear.

Chapter 5 – Home Base

The apartment was empty except for dust, echoes, and the promise of a life.

Third floor. White walls. Terra-cotta tile floors that would be cold in the morning and forgiving in the heat. Two small balconies—one facing the street, one facing the volcano that watched over Antigua like an old, patient god.

"This is it?" Reina asked, standing in the middle of the main room, hands on her hips.

Zeke dropped the duffel bags by the door.

"This is it," he said. "Our very own echo chamber."

She clapped once.

The sound bounced around and came back to them, slightly warped.

"I like the acoustics," she said. "Perfect for arguing and making up."

"Hopefully more of the second," he said.

They signed the lease that would renew in a year that morning. The landlord, a small woman with sharp eyes and a rosary on her wrist, had pressed the keys into Reina's hand like she was passing on a secret.

"Es un buen lugar para empezar de nuevo," she'd said.

It's a good place to start again.

Now, hours later, it still didn't feel entirely real.

Their stuff was on its way: a battered couch from a local resale shop, a small table, a mattress they'd bought from a place Zeke was only eighty percent sure was legitimate. Boxes from Houston would take longer, but the essentials were already stacked downstairs in suitcases, a couple of pots, mismatched mugs, and a Bluetooth speaker.

"Okay," Zeke said, rubbing his palms together. "We have four priorities."

"Oh boy," she said. "Here we go. Engineer brain, activate."

"One," he said, ticking them off. "Get the mattress up here before we die on these tiles."

"Agreed," she said.

"Two," he said. "Figure out how the hot water works, because I love you but I'm not doing cold showers as a lifestyle."

"Fair," she said.

"Three," he said. "Food. We're going to crash if we don't eat soon."

"Also fair," she said. "And four?"

He walked over to his backpack, unzipped it, and pulled out a small, scuffed Bluetooth speaker.

"Four," he said, "we baptize this place properly."

She grinned.

"By the power vested in you by Spotify?" she asked.

"By the order of the universe," he corrected. "And the sacred algorithms."

He set the speaker on the kitchen counter, pulled out his phone, and scrolled.

“Wait,” she said, stepping closer. “We have to do this right.”

He raised an eyebrow. “You have notes?”

“Of course I have notes,” she said. “This is the soundtrack to our new roof.”

She gently took the phone from his hand, opened their shared playlist, and added two songs to the top.

He glanced at the screen.

“Natiruts and MC Magic,” he said. “On brand.”

“I contain multitudes,” she said.

He smiled.

“Hit it, DJ Delgado,” he said.

She tapped play.

A sun-soaked guitar line floated out first, riding on an easy reggae groove. The opening of “I Love” by Natiruts filled the empty room, warm and hopeful.

Zeke’s face changed immediately. His shoulders dropped; his mouth softened.

“This one,” he said, pointing at the speaker like it had said his name. “Always you.”

She felt the words hit that place in her chest that still didn’t entirely trust good things.

“Every time?” she asked.

“Every time,” he said. “Every city. Every room. If ‘I Love’ is playing, it’s dedicated. No need to ask.”

She tried to make a joke and found she couldn’t.

Instead, she stepped into him, into the middle of the room, bare feet on cool tile, music swirling around them.

“Then dance with me, Ali,” she said.

He obliged.

They swayed slowly, awkwardly at first—no choreography, no audience, just two people who’d taken way too long to give themselves this kind of softness. The Portuguese lyrics washed over them. Reina didn’t understand every word, but she understood the feeling.

“I love the way you listen to this song,” she said into his shoulder.

“I love the way this song makes you listen to me,” he said.

“Stop it some more,” she murmured, but there was no resistance in it now. Just a quiet, embarrassing joy.

When the chorus came around again, he gently spun her out and back, almost tripping over an invisible box.

“We need furniture,” he said, laughing.

“We have a floor and music,” she said. “That’s the important part.”

When the last notes faded, he reached over and hit pause before the algorithm could pull something random.

“Now you,” he said. “Your turn.”

She didn’t hesitate.

“Don’t judge me,” she warned, already scrolling.

“You’ve played me every feeling you have over the last two years,” he said. “I’m way past judgment.”

She found it, smiled, and hit play.

The speaker crackled once, then delivered the unmistakable slow-jam synth of MC Magic. A soft voice slid in, talking about a Sexy Lady like she was the only woman on earth.

Zeke groaned.

“Of course,” he said. “The national anthem of Reina Delgado’s teenage heart.”

“You leave MC Magic alone,” she said. “He carried an entire generation of girls with low self-esteem and big hoop earrings.”

“I’m not criticizing,” he said. “I’m observing history.”

She closed her eyes, letting the nostalgia hit. Somewhere in San Antonio, fourteen-year-old Reina was lying on a twin bed, headphones on, dreaming of boys who would never quite understand her.

And here she was now, in Antigua, in a mostly empty apartment with a man who—miracle of miracles—tried.

“This is one of my favorites,” she said softly. “Always has been.”

He stepped closer, smiling.

“I know,” he said. “Every time it comes on, your face does that thing.”

“What thing?” she asked, opening one eye.

"That… soft thing," he said, waving a hand. "Like you remember every crush you ever had and every time you thought you weren't enough, and you finally forgive that girl."

She swallowed.

"That's weirdly accurate," she said.

He took her hand.

"May I have this nostalgic, slightly corny, deeply important dance?" he asked.

"Yes," she said. "You may. But you have to sway correctly. This is sacred slow-jam territory."

"I will defer to the expert," he said.

They moved together again, the MC Magic track wrapping around them like a throwback blanket.

"You know," he said quietly, "if teenage you could see you now…"

"She'd probably ask why it took so long," she said.

"And then," he replied, "she'd see this place, and this playlist, and this man holding you, and go, 'Oh. Worth it.'"

Her throat tightened.

"Stop it some more," she whispered.

He rested his chin on top of her head.

"I'm serious," he said. "You deserved this at fourteen. You deserve it now. You'll deserve it when we're old and Pup is deaf and we're still dancing off-beat in this kitchen."

“You’re assuming we’ll still have this apartment when we’re old,” she said.

“I’m assuming wherever we are, Natiruts and MC Magic are coming with us,” he said. “They’re part of the covenant now.”

She laughed softly at that.

“A covenant above a contract,” she said.

“Exactly,” he said. “We didn’t sign a lease with each other. We signed a playlist.”

“That’s the most millennial thing you’ve ever said,” she replied.

“I’m Gen X,” he protested.

“Playlists are a state of mind,” she said.

He tightened his arms around her.

Outside, a vendor called out about fresh tortillas. Somewhere a dog barked. The volcano sat steady in the distance, like a quiet witness.

Inside, in a room that no longer felt entirely empty, Zeke and Reina let their music choices say the things they still sometimes stumbled over:

I love you the way this song loves the world.

You are my sexy lady, my Reina del Cielo, my partner in the most grown and the most teenage ways.

We are a kaleidoscope that somehow makes one picture.

As the track faded, Reina pulled back and looked around.

“We need a couch,” she said.

“We need plates,” he said. “And curtains.”

“And a dog,” she added absently.

He raised an eyebrow. “One step at a time, Delgado.”

She smiled.

“Fine,” she said. “For now, we have a roof, a view, and a playlist. That’s a pretty good start.”

He nodded, glancing toward the balcony where the first star was just beginning to show.

“Star gazing headquarters,” he said.

“Officially open,” she agreed.

She reached for her phone again.

“One more?” she asked.

He chuckled. “You trying to see how many feelings we can cram into our first night here?”

“Yes,” she said simply.

He exhaled, surrendered, and pulled her close again as the next song started.

Outside, the universe kept its own old rhythm.

Inside, in this new space, their shared beat finally had a roof to echo against.

Final Chapter – Constellations

By the time their second anniversary arrived, the apartment no longer echoed. It sounded like them.

"Look at my little almost-married, not-married people," Rashad had said earlier, hugging them at the door. "Two years of not running away. That's what I call growth."

Now dessert plates were pushed aside, and the evening had softened around the edges.

Zeke cleared his throat.

"I have something," he said, fingers drumming lightly on the table.

Reina eyed him. "If you pull out a ring in your uncle's dining room, I swear—"

"Relax," he cut in. "No rings. We already did our vows in Guatemala, remember? This is... different."

Rashad smirked, clearly entertained. Zeke's mom pretended to be busy in the kitchen but didn't leave the doorway.

Zeke stood, reached into his jacket pocket, and pulled out a small, folded paper.

Reina frowned. "If that's a lease, I'm walking out."

"It's a receipt," he said. "From the vet."

Her breath hitched.

"The vet?" she repeated.

"And the rescue," he added. "They're outside."

He nodded toward the back door.

"Happy anniversary, Reina Delgado," he said. "Year two of star gazing. I thought we could use... one more heart in the constellation."

She pushed her chair back, heart thudding, and all but ran to the back door.

On the small concrete patio, under the porch light, Zeke's mom stood beside a short, soft crate. A tiny black-and-rust Doberman pinscher puppy sat just in front of it, wobbling a little on paws that looked too big for his body.

He was six weeks old. All ears and eyes and clumsy curiosity.

As soon as Reina stepped out, he attempted a brave little bark, promptly lost his balance, and plopped onto his backside.

"Oh my God," she breathed, hands flying to her mouth. "He's a baby."

Zeke came up behind her.

"Six weeks," he said. "They had to bottle-feed him for a bit. Mom's situation was rough. But the rescue lady says he's healthy and stubborn, which... felt on theme."

The pup scrambled back to his feet and toddled unsteadily toward Reina, making its best impression of a metronome on double time.

She crouched down, her dress pooling around her ankles.

"Hi," she whispered. "Hi, little guy."

He sniffed her fingers, then immediately tried to chew on them with comically small teeth.

She laughed, tears already rising.

"He's so tiny," she said. "You didn't tell me he'd be this tiny."

"You would've panicked," Zeke said. "And then accepted him anyway. This way we cut out the pretending."

She scooped the puppy up awkwardly, one hand under his chest, the other supporting his hind legs. He fit against her like he'd rehearsed it.

His little heartbeat thudded against her sternum, faster than it should be, like her own.

"What's his name?" she asked, not taking her eyes off him.

"We can name him whatever you want," Zeke said. "Right now, they've just been calling him 'Pup' at the rescue."

She looked down at the glossy baby face gazing back at her, eyes big and unsure.

"Pup," she said. "You're Pup."

The puppy sneezed once in her direction and then licked her chin.

"See? Agreement," Zeke said.

Reina laughed, the sound wet and bright.

"You got us a dog," she said, still half-disbelieving. "You got me a dog."

"I got us family," he corrected softly. "Another beating heart to share the roof with. Another reason to come home."

Behind them, Rashad stepped onto the porch, mug in hand.

"Oh, Lord," he said. "Y'all got a baby horse."

"He's six weeks," Reina said, pushing to her feet, Pup clutched against her chest. "Be nice."

"I'll be nice," Rashad said. "As long as he doesn't chew on my sax reeds. Or my shoes. Or my soul."

Pup yawned hugely in his direction, unimpressed.

Zeke slipped an arm around Reina's waist, careful not to jostle the puppy.

"Happy anniversary," he murmured in her ear.

She leaned into him, Pup squirming lightly between them.

"You are too beautiful for words to describe you, señor Ali," she said. "For real."

"Stop it some more," he replied, grinning.

Pup let out a tiny, confused woof, as if trying to learn the language of whatever this was.

Reina buried her face briefly in the puppy's soft neck, inhaling that warm, milky puppy smell she hadn't realized she'd missed her whole life.

"Welcome to the covenant, Pup," she whispered. "No contracts. Just us."

—

Months passed the way good months do—quietly, quickly, marked less by drama than by rhythm. By the time they were back on the rooftop in Antigua, Pup had grown into his paws just enough to believe the whole world belonged to him.

Reina scratched his chest absentmindedly, looking out over the tiled roofs and the volcano outlined against a deepening indigo sky.

“You realize we’re ridiculous,” she said.

“How so?” Zeke asked, stretching his legs out, bare feet brushing the dog’s flank.

“Two middle-aged, non-married, long-distance reformed commitment-phobes, splitting time between countries with a rescued Doberman named Pup,” she said. “This is not in any relationship handbook I’ve ever seen.”

“Good,” he said. “Most handbooks are boring.”

Below, the sounds of the city blended into a familiar hum. Someone’s radio played an old ballad in Spanish. A kid laughed. A scooter passed. Somewhere, a dog barked in response to Pup’s earlier yawn.

Zeke checked his phone and smiled.

“Tasha sends her love,” he said. “And a photo of her new office.”

Reina leaned over to look. The picture showed Tasha in a glass-walled space with a plant that was obviously thriving, a whiteboard full of scribbles, and a plaque that said Director of People & Culture.

“She did it,” Reina said softly. “She got out.”

“She says,” Zeke read, “‘Tell Reina I finally work somewhere that understands boundaries and doesn’t use pizza parties as trauma patches.’”

Reina laughed, heart swelling.

"What about Miri?" she asked.

Zeke scrolled. "Sent a voice note."

He hit play. Miri's voice crackled through, all warmth and mischief.

"Reporting live from San Antonio, where your girl just turned down a man because he gave me Antonio vibes. Growth! Also, my new guy brings his own umbrella. Figuratively. We're taking it slowly. I'm good. I love you. Pet Pup for me. Tell Zeke he's lucky and tell Reina to stop it some more."

Reina shook her head, smiling so hard it almost hurt.

"She's really okay," she said.

"She's really okay," he echoed.

His phone buzzed again. A text from his mom: Your uncle says hi. He made the freshmen listen to Kind of Blue three times this week. Says it's good for their souls.

Right under it, a photo: Rashad at the front of his classroom, sax in hand, Pup's spare chew toy inexplicably sitting on the windowsill behind him like some strange little blessing.

Reina took the phone, zoomed in, and laughed.

"He stole our dog's toy for his class," she said.

"Object lesson," Zeke said. "'Even the chewed-up things have music in them,' or something."

She went quiet for a moment, watching the last of the sun slide behind the mountains.

“Do you ever... miss the version of your life where this never happened?” she asked. “No me. No Guatemala. No Pup. Just... you in Houston, playing it safe.”

He thought about it.

“No,” he said honestly. “I miss the simplicity sometimes. But not the smallness.”

He turned to look at her.

“What about you?” he asked. “You ever miss the version where you stayed director, climbed the ladder, married some safe guy in San Antonio, never got on that flight?”

She let the question sit between them.

“Sometimes I miss the illusion of control,” she said. “My old calendar made sense. My paychecks were predictable. My LinkedIn was smug.”

“And now?” he asked.

“And now my heart is louder,” she said. “My nervous system is kinder. My passport is dirtier. My work feels like mine. And I get to wake up next to a man who compliments me so much I’ve had to invent new grammar to handle it.”

“Stop it some more,” he said automatically, then caught himself. “Wait, that’s your line.”

She laughed.

“Advanced English,” she reminded him.

Pup let out a long, contented sigh, thumping his tail once against Zeke’s foot.

"You know he was terrified when we brought him home," Zeke said. "Every sound made him jump. Every time I picked up my keys, he thought I was leaving forever."

"Same," Reina said dryly.

He gave her a look.

"I'm kidding," she said. "Mostly."

Zeke reached over, resting his hand on her knee.

"He still flinches sometimes," Zeke said, nodding at the dog. "Loud noises. Sudden movements. But look at him now. Rooftop in Guatemala, full belly, family on both continents. He has no idea how strange and lucky his life is."

Reina watched Pup, then looked at Zeke.

"We're all rescues," she said quietly.

He smiled.

"You are too beautiful for words to describe you, señorita Delgado," he said again, softer this time, not just about her face or her dress, but about the whole of her—scars, laughter, affirmations, and all.

She felt the compliment land differently now than it used to.

Less like an attack. More like a mirror she was finally willing to look into.

"Stop it some more," she whispered.

She turned toward him, their shoulders touching as the first stars appeared overhead.

They lay back on the blanket, Pup repositioning himself with a grunt so that he blocked half of Reina's view of the sky. She scratched his ear anyway.

"Do you think this is it?" she asked. "Our end of the story?"

"No," Zeke said. "But I think this is the end of this chapter. The 'can we even do this' chapter. From here on out, it's just... living it."

She nodded.

Above them, constellations slowly sharpened in the dark—familiar shapes they were still learning the names of.

Below, their little constellation—Reina, Zeke, Pup, Miri, Tasha, Rashad, her parents, his mom, two cities, one messy, precious life—glowed in its own, imperfect way.

Reina glanced sideways at him.

"Thank you," she said.

"For what?" he asked.

"For playing the hand, you have," she said. "For not folding when it got weird. For asking me to stop it some more until I believed you."

He swallowed, throat thick.

"Thank you for being the hand I have," he said. "For being my Reina del Cielo and my Reina del Chaos. For splitting a life with me instead of making me choose which part to keep."

She reached over, laced their fingers together.

"Look, Pup," she said softly, pointing up. "Stars. That's what your humans do. We stare at them and make our lives into shapes."

The puppy—still a puppy at heart—huffed, unconcerned, and laid his head across both their legs.

Zeke squeezed her hand.

"Star gazing," he said.

"Always," she replied.

They lay there under the Guatemalan sky, under Houston's echoes, under all the almost-meetings they'd survived and all the flights still ahead. Two people who had finally learned to coexist tangibly—one roof here, roots there, all twelve months fully themselves.

Author's Note

I would like to first and foremost thank Frank Ocean. Listening to channel ORANGE kept my mind tuned to the creative vibrations I needed to stay connected to the life, characters, and heartbeat of this creation. There is a peace that has come from writing Star Gazing in Guatemala. I am forever thankful for the inspirations that allowed me to manifest this. I offer a sincere thank you to the smiles and joys, and to the sadness and disappointments of life that I could not have written without.

I didn't set out to write a love story. I sat down with a feeling. It started as this ache: what happens to us when we've lived enough life to have regrets, scars, and bills—but we still want something real? Do we get to have passion and safety? Can we build something true after divorce, burnout, or bad choices, or is that just for people who are younger, lighter, and less complicated?

Zeke and Reina showed up in that question.

They carry pieces of people I've seen and loved: the woman holding everybody else together while secretly falling apart; the man who is funny and dependable but afraid to say what he really feels; the uncle who has made peace with his past and still wants better for the next generation; the friends who see us clearly even when we can't.

Guatemala is more than a backdrop here. It's a kind of mirror. I wanted a place where the sky feels close, where streets are older than our timelines, where you can stand on a rooftop and feel both very small and very held. For these characters, Guatemala became the setting where they could finally hear themselves—and each other—without all the noise.

Music runs through this book on purpose. We are all, in some way, the songs that raised us. Natiruts, MC Magic, jazz records, late-night playlists—those are the languages some of us learned to feel in long before we had therapy words. It felt honest to let these characters speak in chords and chorus when regular sentences weren't enough.

Most of all, this is a book about covenant over contract.

There's no fairy-tale wedding here. No perfect bow. Just two people choosing each other again and again without guarantees, without pretending it's easy, and without waiting to be "fixed" first. They don't get the hand they thought they wanted. They get the hand they have—and they learn to play it with as much honesty and tenderness as they can.

If you see yourself in any of them, that's not an accident. It doesn't mean you are them. It means you're human, too.

Thank you for spending time with this constellation of people and places. My hope is that somewhere in these pages, you feel a little less alone, a little more willing to look up at your own sky, and maybe a little more open to a love that is messy, late, and exactly right on time.

—Elias Shabazz

www.ingramcontent.com/pod-product-compliance
Lightning Source LLC
LaVergne TN
LVHW020640100826
845148LV00012B/2270

* 9 7 9 8 2 3 4 0 5 8 6 4 5 *